Elizabeth Barrett Browning

Elizabeth Barrett Browning's Poetical Works

Volume 1

Elizabeth Barrett Browning

Elizabeth Barrett Browning's Poetical Works
Volume 1

ISBN/EAN: 9783337142131

Printed in Europe, USA, Canada, Australia, Japan

Cover: Foto ©Andreas Hilbeck / pixelio.de

More available books at **www.hansebooks.com**

POEMS

ELIZABETH BARRETT BROWNING'S

POETICAL WORKS.

TWELFTH EDITION.

IN FIVE VOLUMES.

VOL. I.

LONDON:

SMITH, ELDER, & CO., 15 WATERLOO PLACE.

1889

Dedication.

—◆—

TO MY FATHER.

WHEN your eyes fall upon this page of dedication, and you start to see to whom it is inscribed, your first thought will be of the time far off when I was a child and wrote verses, and when I dedicated them to you who were my public and my critic. Of all that such a recollection implies of saddest and sweetest to both of us, it would become neither of us to speak before the world; nor would it be possible for us to speak of it to one another, with voices that did not falter. Enough, that what is in my heart when I write thus, will be fully known to yours.

And my desire is that you, who are a witness how if this art of poetry had been a less earnest object to me, it must have fallen from exhausted hands before this day,—that you, who have shared with me in things bitter and sweet, softening or enhancing them, every day,—that you, who hold with me over all sense of loss and transiency, one hope by one Name,—may accept from me the inscription of these volumes, the exponents of a few years of an existence which has been sustained and comforted by you as well as given. Somewhat more faint-hearted than I used to be, it is my fancy thus to seem to return to a visible personal dependence on you, as if indeed I were a child again; to conjure your beloved image between myself and the public, so as to be sure of one smile,—and to satisfy my heart while I sanctify my ambition, by associating with the great pursuit of my life, its tenderest and holiest affection.

Your

E. B. B.

London, 50, Wimpole Street.
1844.

ADVERTISEMENT.

THIS edition, including my earlier and later writings, I have endeavoured to render as little unworthy as possible of the indulgence of the public. Several poems I would willingly have withdrawn, if it were not almost impossible to extricate what has been once caught and involved in the machinery of the press. The alternative is a request to the generous reader that he may use the weakness of those earlier verses, which no subsequent revision has succeeded in strengthening, less as a reproach to the writer, than as a means of marking some progress in her other attempts.

E. B. B.

LONDON, 1856.

CONTENTS.

———◇———

A DRAMA OF EXILE.

E

A DRAMA OF EXILE.

———◆———

SCENE.—*The outer side of the gate of Eden shut fast with cloud,
from the depth of which revolves a sword of fire self-moved.
ADAM and EVE are seen in the distance flying along the glare.*

LUCIFER, *alone.*

REJOICE in the clefts of Gehenna,
  My exiled, my host!
Earth has exiles as hopeless as when a
  Heaven's empire was lost.
Through the seams of her shaken foundations,
  Smoke up in great joy!
With the smoke of your fierce exultations
  Deform and destroy!
Smoke up with your lurid revenges,
  And darken the face
Of the white heavens and taunt them with changes
  From glory and grace.
We, in falling, while destiny strangles,
  Pull down with us all.
Let them look to the rest of their angels!
  Who's safe from a fall?

B 2

HE saves not. Where's Adam? Can pardon
   Requicken that sod?
Unkinged is the King of the Garden,
   The image of God.
Other exiles are cast out of Eden,—
   More curse has been hurled:
Come up, O my locusts, and feed in
   The green of the world!
Come up! we have conquered by evil;
   Good reigns not alone:
I prevail now, and, angel or devil,
   Inherit a throne.

   [*In sudden apparition a watch of innumerable angels, rank
    above rank, slopes up from around the gate to the zenith.
    The angel* GABRIEL *descends.*

Luc. Hail Gabriel, the keeper of the gate!
Now that the fruit is plucked, prince Gabriel,
I hold that Eden is impregnable
Under thy keeping.
   Gab.   Angel of the sin,
Such as thou standest,—pale in the drear light
Which rounds the rebel's work with Maker's wrath,—
Thou shalt be an Idea to all souls,
A monumental melancholy gloom
Seen down all ages, whence to mark despair
And measure out the distances from good.
Go from us straightway!
   Luc.   Wherefore?
   Gab.   Lucifer,

Thy last step in this place trod sorrow up.
Recoil before that sorrow, if not this sword.

Luc. Angels are in the world—wherefore not I?
Exiles are in the world—wherefore not I?
The cursed are in the world—wherefore not I?

Gab. Depart!

Luc. And where's the logic of 'depart'?
Our lady Eve had half been satisfied
To obey her Maker, if I had not learnt
To fix my postulate better.   Dost thou dream
Of guarding some monopoly in heaven
Instead of earth?   Why, I can dream with thee
To the length of thy wings.

Gab. I do not dream.
This is not heaven, even in a dream, nor earth,
As earth was once, first breathed among the stars,
Articulate glory from the mouth divine,
To which the myriad spheres thrilled audibly,
Touched like a lute-string, and the sons of God
Said AMEN, singing it.   I know that this
Is earth not new created but new cursed—
This, Eden's gate not opened but built up
With a final cloud of sunset.   Do I dream?
Alas, not so! this is the Eden lost
By Lucifer the serpent; this the sword
(This sword alive with justice and with fire)
That smote upon the forehead, Lucifer
The angel.   Wherefore, angel, go—depart!
Enough is sinned and suffered.

Luc.   By no means.
Here's a brave earth to sin and suffer on:
It holds fast still—it cracks not under curse;
It holds like mine immortal.   Presently
We'll sow it thick enough with graves as green
Or greener certes, than its knowledge-tree.
We'll have the cypress for the tree of life,
More eminent for shadow: for the rest,
We'll build it dark with towns and pyramids,
And temples, if it please you:—we'll have feasts
And funerals also, merrymakes and wars,
Till blood and wine shall mix and run along
Right o'er the edges.   And, good Gabriel,
(Ye like that word in heaven) *I* too have strength—
Strength to behold Him and not worship Him,
Strength to fall from Him and not cry on Him,
Strength to be in the universe and yet
Neither God nor his servant.   The red sign
Burnt on my forehead, which you taunt me with,
Is God's sign that it bows not unto God,
The potter's mark upon his work, to show
It rings well to the striker.   I and the earth
Can bear more curse.

    Gab.   O miserable earth,
O ruined angel!

    Luc.   Well, and if it be!
I CHOSE this ruin; I elected it
Of my will, not of service.   What I do,
I do volitient, not obedient,

And overtop thy crown with my despair.
My sorrow crowns me. Get thee back to heaven,
And leave me to the earth, which is mine own
In virtue of her ruin, as I hers
In virtue of my revolt! turn thou from both
That bright, impassive, passive angelhood,
And spare to read us backward any more
Of the spent hallelujahs!

    Gab.   Spirit of scorn,
I might say, of unreason! I might say,
That who despairs, acts; that who acts, connives
With God's relations set in time and space;
That who elects, assumes a something good
Which God made possible; that who lives, obeys
The law of a Life-maker . . .

    Luc.   Let it pass!
No more, thou Gabriel! What if I stand up
And strike my brow against the crystalline
Roofing the creatures,—shall I say, for that,
My stature is too high for me to stand,—
Henceforward I must sit? Sit *thou*!

    Gab.   I kneel.

    Luc. A heavenly answer. Get thee to thy heaven,
And leave my earth to me!

    Gab.   Through heaven and earth
God's will moves freely, and I follow it,
As colour follows light. He overflows
The firmamental walls with deity,
Therefore with love; His lightnings go abroad,

His pity may do so, His angels must,
Whene'er He gives them charges.

    Luc.   Verily,
I and my demons, who are spirits of scorn,
Might hold this charge of standing with a sword
'Twixt man and his inheritance, as well
As the benignest angel of you all.

    Gab. Thou speakest in the shadow of thy change.
If thou hadst gazed upon the face of God
This morning for a moment, thou hadst known
That only pity fitly can chastise.
Hate but avenges.

    Luc.   As it is, I know
Something of pity. When I reeled in heaven,
And my sword grew too heavy for my grasp,
Stabbing through matter, which it could not pierce
So much as the first shell of,—toward the throne;
When I fell back, down,—staring up as I fell,—
The lightnings holding open my scathed lids,
And that thought of the infinite of God,
Hurled after to precipitate descent;
When countless angel faces still and stern
Pressed out upon me from the level heavens
Adown the abysmal spaces, and I fell
Trampled down by your stillness, and struck blind
By the sight within your eyes,—'twas then I knew
How ye could pity, my kind angelhood!

    Gab. Alas, discrowned one, by the truth in me
Which God keeps in me, I would give away

All—save that truth and His love keeping it,—
To lead thee home again into the light
And hear thy voice chant with the morning stars,
When their rays tremble round them with much song
Sung in more gladness!

    Luc.   Sing, my Morning Star!
Last beautiful, last heavenly, that I loved!
If I could drench thy golden locks with tears,
What were it to this angel?

    Gab.   What love is.
And now I have named God.

    Luc.   Yet, Gabriel,
By the lie in me which I keep myself,
Thou'rt a false swearer. Were it otherwise,
What dost thou here, vouchsafing tender thoughts
To that earth-angel or earth-demon—which,
Thou and I have not solved the problem yet
Enough to argue,—that fallen Adam there,—
That red-clay and a breath,—who must, forsooth,
Live in a new apocalypse of sense,
With beauty and music waving in his trees
And running in his rivers, to make glad
His soul made perfect?—is it not for hope,
A hope within thee deeper than thy truth,
Of finally conducting him and his
To fill the vacant thrones of me and mine,
Which affront heaven with their vacuity?

    Gab. Angel, there are no vacant thrones in heaven
To suit thy empty words. Glory and life

Fulfil their own depletions; and if God
Sighed you far from Him, His next breath drew in
A compensative splendour up the vast,
Flushing the starry arteries.

    Luc.   With a change!
So, let the vacant thrones and gardens too
Fill as may please you!—and be pitiful,
As ye translate that word, to the dethroned
And exiled, man or angel.   The fact stands,
That I, the rebel, the cast out and down,
Am here and will not go; while there, along
The light to which ye flash the desert out,
Flies your adopted Adam, your red-clay
In two kinds, both being flawed.   Why, what is this?
Whose work is this?   Whose hand was in the work?
Against whose hand?   In this last strife, methinks,
I am not a fallen angel!

    Gab.   Dost thou know
Aught of those exiles?

    Luc.   Ay: I know they have fled
Silent all day along the wilderness:
I know they wear, for burden on their backs,
The thought of a shut gate of Paradise,
And faces of the marshalled cherubim
Shining against, not for them; and I know
They dare not look in one another's face,—
As if each were a cherub!

    Gab.   **Dost thou know**
Aught of their future?

Luc.   Only as much as this:
That evil will increase and multiply
Without a benediction.

    Gab.   Nothing more?

    Luc. Why so the angels taunt! What should be more?

    Gab. God is more.

    Luc.   Proving what?

    Gab.   That He is God,
And capable of saving. Lucifer,
I charge thee by the solitude He kept
Ere he created,—leave the earth to God!

    Luc. My foot is on the earth, firm as my sin.

    Gab. I charge thee by the memory of heaven
Ere any sin was done,—leave earth to God!

    Luc. My sin is on the earth, to reign thereon.

    Gab. I charge thee by the choral song we sang,
When up against the white shore of our feet,
The depths of the creation swelled and brake,—
And the new worlds, the beaded foam and flower
Of all that coil, roared outward into space
On thunder-edges,—leave the earth to God!

    Luc. My woe is on the earth, to curse thereby.

    Gab. I charge thee by that mournful Morning Star
Which trembles . . . .

    Luc.   Enough spoken. As the pine
In norland forest, drops its weight of snows
By a night's growth, so, growing toward my ends
I drop thy counsels. Farewell, Gabriel!
Watch out thy service; I achieve my will.

And peradventure in the after years,
When thoughtful men shall bend their spacious brows
Upon the storm and strife seen everywhere
To ruffle their smooth manhood and break up
With lurid lights of intermittent hope
Their human fear and wrong,—they may discern
The heart of a lost angel in the earth

CHORUS OF EDEN SPIRITS,

(Chanting from Paradise, while ADAM *and* EVE *fly across
the Sword-glare.)*

Harken, oh harken! let your souls behind you
　　　　Turn, gently moved!
Our voices feel along the Dread to find you,
　　　　O lost, beloved!
Through the thick-shielded and strong-marshalled
　　　　angels,
　　　　They press and pierce:
Our requiems follow fast on our evangels,—
　　　　Voice throbs in verse.
We are but orphaned spirits left in Eden
　　　　A time ago:
God gave us golden cups, and we were bidden
　　　　To feed you so.
But now our right hand hath no cup remaining,
　　　　No work to do,

The mystic hydromel is spilt, and staining
    The whole earth through.
Most ineradicable stains, for showing
    (Not interfused!)
That brighter colours were the world's foregoing,
    Than shall be used.
Harken, oh harken! ye shall harken surely
    For years and years,
The noise beside you, dripping coldly, purely,
    Of spirits' tears.
The yearning to a beautiful denied you,
    Shall strain your powers.
Ideal sweetnesses shall over-glide you,
    Resumed from ours.
In all your music, our pathetic minor
    Your ears shall cross;
And all good gifts shall mind you of diviner,
    With sense of loss.
We shall be near you in your poet-languors
    And wild extremes,
What time ye vex the desert with vain angers,
    Or mock with dreams.
And when upon you, weary after roaming,
    Death's seal is put,
By the foregone ye shall discern the coming,
    Through eyelids shut.
Spirits of the trees.
    Hark! the Eden trees are stirring,
    Soft and solemn in your hearing!

Oak and linden, palm and fir,
Tamarisk and juniper,
Each still throbbing in vibration
Since that crowning of creation
When the God-breath spake abroad,
Let us make man like to God!
And the pine stood quivering
    As the awful word went by,
Like a vibrant music-string
    Stretched from mountain-peak to sky;
And the platan did expand
    Slow and gradual, branch and head;
    And the cedar's strong black shade
Fluttered brokenly and grand:
Grove and wood were swept aslant
In emotion jubilant.

Voice of the same, but softer.

Which divine impulsion cleaves
In dim movements to the leaves
Dropt and lifted, dropt and lifted
In the sunlight greenly sifted,—
In the sunlight and the moonlight
    Greenly sifted through the trees.
    Ever wave the Eden trees
In the nightlight and the noonlight.
With a ruffling of green branches
Shaded off to resonances,
    Never stirred by rain or breeze.
Fare ye well, farewell!

The sylvan sounds, no longer audible,
Expire at Eden's door.
  Each footstep of your treading
Treads out some murmur which ye heard before.
  Farewell! the trees of Eden
Ye shall hear nevermore.

River-spirits.

  Hark! the flow of the four rivers—
    Hark the flow!
  How the silence round you shivers,
    While our voices through it go,
  Cold and clear.

A softer voice.

  Think a little, while ye hear,
    Of the banks
  Where the willows and the deer
    Crowd in intermingled ranks,
  As if all would drink at once
  Where the living water runs!—
    Of the fishes' golden edges
    Flashing in and out the sedges;
  Of the swans on silver thrones,
    Floating down the winding streams
  With impassive eyes turned shoreward
  And a chant of undertones,—
  And the lotos leaning forward
    To help them into dreams!
  Fare ye well, farewell!
  The river-sounds, no longer audible.

Expire at Eden's door.
Each footstep of your treading
Treads out some murmur which ye heard before.
Farewell! the streams of Eden,
Ye shall hear nevermore.

Bird-spirit.

I am the nearest nightingale
That singeth in Eden after you;
And I am singing loud and true,
And sweet,—I do not fail.
I sit upon a cypress bough,
Close to the gate, and I fling my song
Over the gate and through the mail
Of the warden angels marshalled strong,—
Over the gate and after you.
And the warden angels let it pass,
Because the poor brown bird, alas,
Sings in the garden, sweet and true.
And I build my song of high pure notes,
Note over note, height over height,
Till I strike the arch of the Infinite,
And I bridge abysmal agonies
With strong, clear calms of harmonies,—
And something abides, and something floats,
In the song which I sing after you.
Fare ye well, farewell!
The creature-sounds, no longer audible,
Expire at Eden's door.
Each footstep of your treading

Treads out some cadence which ye heard before.

      Farewell! the birds of Eden,
      Ye shall hear nevermore.

Flower-spirits.

We linger, we linger,
    The last of the throng,
Like the tones of a singer
    Who loves his own song.
We are spirit-aromas
    Of blossom and bloom.
We call your thoughts home,—as
    Ye breathe our perfume,—
To the amaranth's splendour
    Afire on the slopes;
To the lily-bells tender,
    And grey heliotropes;
To the poppy-plains keeping
    Such dream-breath and blee
That the angels there stepping
    Grew whiter to see:
To the nook, set with moly,
    Ye jested one day in,
Till your smile waxed too holy
    And left your lips praying:
To the rose in the bower-place,
    That dripped o'er you sleeping;
To the asphodel flower-place,
    Ye walked ankle-deep in.
We pluck at your raiment,

We stroke down your hair,
We faint in our lament
And pine into air.
Fare ye well, farewell!
The Eden scents, no longer sensible,
Expire at Eden's door.
Each footstep of your treading
Treads out some fragrance which ye knew **before**.
Farewell! the flowers of Eden,
Ye shall smell nevermore.

[*There is silence.* ADAM *and* EVE *fly on, and never look back.
Only a colossal shadow, as of the dark* Angel *passing
quickly, is cast upon the Sword-glare.*

SCENE.—*The extremity of the Sword-glare.*

Adam. Pausing a moment on this outer edge
Where the supernal sword-glare cuts in light
The dark exterior desert,—hast thou strength,
Beloved, to look behind us to the gate?
Eve. Have I not strength to look up to thy face?
Adam. We need be strong: yon spectacle of cloud
Which seals the gate up to the final doom,
Is God's seal manifest. There seem to lie
A hundred thunders in it, dark and dead;
The unmolten lightnings vein it motionless;
And, outward from its depth, the self-moved sword
Swings slow its awful gnomon of red fire

From side to side, in pendulous horror slow,
Across the stagnant ghastly glare thrown flat
On the intermediate ground from that to this.
The angelic hosts, the archangelic pomps,
Throues, dominations, princedoms, rank on rank,
Rising sublimely to the feet of God,
On either side and overhead the gate,
Show like a glittering and sustainĕd smoke
Drawn to an apex.   That their faces shine
Betwixt the solemn clasping of their wings
Clasped high to a silver point above their heads,—
We only guess from hence, and not discern.

   Eve. Though we were near enough to see them shine,
The shadow on thy face were awfuller,
To me, at least,—to me—than all their light.

   Adam. What is this, Eve? thou droppest heavily
In a heap earthward, and thy body heaves
Under the golden floodings of thine hair!

   Eve. O Adam, Adam! by that name of Eve—
Thine Eve, thy life—which suits me little now,
Seeing that I now confess myself thy death
And thine undoer, as the snake was mine,—
I do adjure thee, put me straight away,
Together with my name! Sweet, punish me!
O Love, be just! and, ere we pass beyond
The light cast outward by the fiery sword,
Into the dark which earth must be to us,
Bruise my head with thy foot,—as the curse said
My seed shall the first tempter's! strike with curse,

As God struck in the garden! and as HE,
Being satisfied with justice and with wrath,
Did roll His thunder gentler at the close,—
Thou, peradventure, may'st at last recoil
To some soft need of mercy.   Strike, my lord!
I, also, after tempting, writhe on the ground,
And I would feed on ashes from thine hand,
As suits me, O my tempted!
   Adam.   My beloved,
Mine Eve and life—I have no other name
For thee or for the sun than what ye are,
My utter life and light!   If we have fallen,
It is that we have sinned,—we: God is just;
And, since His curse doth comprehend us both,
It must be that His balance holds the weights
Of first and last sin on a level.   What!
Shall I who had not virtue to stand straight
Among the hills of Eden, here assume
To mend the justice of the perfect God,
By piling up a curse upon His curse,
Against thee—thee?
   Eve.   For so, perchance, thy God,
Might take thee into grace for scorning me;
Thy wrath against the sinner giving proof
Of inward abrogation of the sin:
And so, the blessed angels might come down
And walk with thee as erst,—I think they would,—
Because I was not near to make them sad
Or soil the rustling of their innocence.

Adam. They know me. I am deepest in the guilt,
If last in the transgression.

  Eve.   Thou!

  Adam.   If God,
Who gave the right and joyaunce of the world
Both unto thee and me,—gave thee to me,
The best gift last, the last sin was the worst,
Which sinned against more complement of gifts
And grace of giving. God! I render back
Strong benediction and perpetual praise
From mortal feeble lips (as incense-smoke,
Out of a little censer, may fill heaven),
That Thou, in striking my benumbëd hands
And forcing them to drop all other boons
Of beauty and dominion and delight,—
Hast left this well-beloved Eve, this life
Within life, this best gift between their palms,
In gracious compensation!

  Eve.   Is it thy voice?
Or some saluting angel's—calling home
My feet into the garden?

  Adam.   O my God!
I, standing here between the glory and dark,—
The glory of thy wrath projected forth
From Eden's wall, the dark of our distress
Which settles a step off in that drear world—
Lift up to Thee the hands from whence hath fallen
Only creation's sceptre,—thanking Thee
That rather Thou hast cast me out with *her*

Than left me lorn of her in Paradise,
With angel looks and angel songs around
To show the absence of her eyes and voice,
And make society full desertness
Without her use in comfort!

   Eve.   Where is loss?
Am I in Eden? can another speak
Mine own love's tongue?

   Adam.   Because with *her*, I stand
Upright, as far as can be in this fall,
And look away from heaven which doth accuse,
And look away from earth which doth convict,
Into her face, and crown my discrowned brow
Out of her love, and put the thought of her
Around me, for an Eden full of birds,
And lift her body up—thus—to my heart,
And with my lips upon her lips,—thus, thus,—
Do quicken and sublimate my mortal breath
Which cannot climb against the grave's steep sides
But overtops this grief!

   Eve.   I am renewed.
My eyes grow with the light which is in thine;
The silence of my heart is full of sound.
Hold me up—so! Because I comprehend
This human love, I shall not be afraid
Of any human death; and yet because
I know this strength of love, I seem to know
Death's strength by that same sign. Kiss on my lips,
To shut the door close on my rising soul,—

Lest it pass outwards in astonishment
And leave thee lonely !

   Adam.   Yet thou liest, Eve,
Bent heavily on thyself across mine arm,
Thy face flat to the sky.

   Eve.   Ay, and the tears
Running, as it might seem, my life from me,
They run so fast and warm. Let me lie so,
And weep so, as if in a dream or prayer,
Unfastening, clasp by clasp, the hard tight thought
Which clipped my heart and showed me evermore
Loathed of thy justice as I loathe the snake,
And as the pure ones loathe our sin. To-day,
All day, beloved, as we fled across
This desolating radiance cast by swords
Not suns,—my lips prayed soundless to myself,
Striking against each other—' O Lord God!'
('Twas so I prayed) ' I ask Thee by my sin,
' And by Thy curse, and by Thy blameless heavens,
' Make dreadful haste to hide me from Thy face
' And from the face of my beloved here
' For whom I am no helpmeet, quick away
' Into the new dark mystery of death!
' I will lie still there, I will make no plaint,
' I will not sigh, nor sob, nor speak a word,
' Nor struggle to come back beneath the sun
' Where peradventure I might sin anew
' Against Thy mercy and his pleasure. Death,
' Oh death, whate'er it be, is good enough

'For such as I am: while for Adam here.
'No voice shall say again, in heaven or earth,
' *It is not good for him to be alone.*'

   Adam. And was it good for such a prayer to pass,
My unkind Eve, betwixt our mutual lives?
If I am exiled, must I be bereaved?

   Eve. 'Twas an ill prayer: it shall be prayed no more;
And God did use it like a foolishness,
Giving no answer. Now my heart has grown
Too high and strong for such a foolish prayer;
Love makes it strong: and since I was the first
In the transgression, with a steady foot
I will be first to tread from this sword-glare
Into the outer darkness of the waste,—
And thus I do it.

   Adam.   Thus I follow thee,
As erewhile in the sin —What sounds! what sounds!
I feel a music which comes straight from heaven,
As tender as a watering dew.

   Eve.   I think
That angels—not those guarding Paradise,—
But the love-angels, who came erst to us,
And when we said 'GOD,' fainted unawares
Back from our mortal presence unto God,
(As if He drew them inward in a breath)
His name being heard of them,—I think that they
With sliding voices lean from heavenly towers,
Invisible but gracious. Hark—how soft!

CHORUS OF **INVISIBLE** ANGELS.

Faint and tender.

Mortal **man and** woman,
  Go upon your travel!
Heaven assist the human
  Smoothly to unravel
All that web of pain
  Wherein ye are holden.
Do ye know our voices
  Chanting down the Golden?
Do ye guess our choice is,
  Being unbeholden,
To be harkened by you yet again?

This pure door of opal
  God hath shut between us,—
Us, his shining people,
  You, who once have seen us
And are blinded new!
  Yet, across the doorway,
Past the silence reaching,
  Farewells evermore may,
Blessing in the teaching,
  Glide from us to you.

First semichorus.

  Think how erst your Eden,
Day on day succeeding,

With our presence glowed.
We came as if the Heavens were bowed
   To a milder music rare.
Ye saw us in our solemn treading,
   Treading down the steps of cloud,
While our wings, outspreading
   Double calms of whiteness,
   Dropped superfluous brightness
   Down from stair to stair.

Second semichorus.

   Or oft, abrupt though tender,
      While ye gazed on space,
   We flashed our angel-splendour
      In either human face.
With mystic lilies in our hands,
From the atmospheric bands
      Breaking with a sudden grace,
We took you unaware!
   While our feet struck glories
Outward, smooth and fair,
   Which we stood on floorwise,
Platformed in mid-air.

First semichorus.

   Or oft, when Heaven-descended,
      Stood we in our wondering sight
   In a mute apocalypse
   With dumb vibrations on our lips
From hosannas ended,
   And grand half-vanishings

Of the empyreal things
  Within our eyes belated,
Till the heavenly Infinite
  Falling off from the Created,
Left our inward contemplation
Opened into ministration.

Chorus.

Then upon our axle turning
  Of great joy to sympathy,
We sang out the morning
  Broadening up the sky.
Or we drew
Our music through
The noontide's hush and heat and shine,
Informed with our intense Divine!
Interrupted vital notes
  Palpitating hither, thither,
  Burning out into the æther,
Sensible like fiery motes.
Or, whenever twilight drifted
  Through the cedar masses,
The globëd sun we lifted,
Trailing purple, trailing gold
  Out between the passes
Of the mountains manifold,
To anthems slowly sung!
While he, aweary, half in swoon
For joy to hear our climbing tune
  Transpierce the stars' concentric rings,—

The burden of his glory flung
  In broken lights upon our wings.

[*The chant dies away confusedly, and* LUCIFER *appears.*

Luc. Now may all fruits be pleasant to thy lips,
Beautiful Eve! The times have somewhat changed
Since thou and I had talk beneath a tree,
Albeit ye are not gods yet.

Eve.   Adam! hold
My right hand strongly! It is Lucifer—
And we have love to lose.

Adam.   I' the name of God,
Go apart from us, O thou Lucifer!
And leave us to the desert thou hast made
Out of thy treason. Bring no serpent-slime
Athwart this path kept holy to our tears!
Or we may curse thee with their bitterness.

Luc. Curse freely! curses thicken. Why, this Eve
Who thought me once part worthy of her ear
And somewhat wiser than the other beasts,—
Drawing together her large globes of eyes,
The light of which is throbbing in and out
Their steadfast continuity of gaze,—
Knots her fair eyebrows in so hard a knot,
And down from her white heights of womanhood
Looks on me so amazed,—I scarce should fear
To wager such an apple as she plucked,
Against one riper from the tree of life,
That she could curse too—as a woman may—
Smooth in the vowels.

Eve.   So—speak wickedly!
I like it best so.   Let thy words be wounds,—
For, so, I shall not fear thy power to hurt.
Trench on the forms of good by open ill—
For, so, I shall wax strong and grand with scorn,
Scorning myself for ever trusting thee
As far as thinking, ere a snake ate dust,
He could speak wisdom.

Luc.   Our new gods, it seems,
Deal more in thunders than in courtesies.
And, sooth, mine own Olympus, which anon
I shall build up to loud-voiced imagery
From all the wandering visions of the world,
May show worse railing than our lady Eve
Pours o'er the rounding of her argent arm.
But why should this be ?   Adam pardoned Eve.

Adam. Adam loved Eve.   Jehovah pardon both!

Eve. Adam forgave Eve—because loving Eve.

Luc. So, well.   Yet Adam was undone of Eve,
As both were by the snake.   Therefore forgive,
In like wise, fellow-temptress, the poor snake—
Who stung there, not so poorly !   [*Aside.*

Eve.   Hold thy wrath,
Beloved Adam ! let me answer him ;
For this time he speaks truth, which we should hear,
And asks for mercy, which I most should grant,
In like wise, as he tells us—in like wise !
And therefore I thee pardon, Lucifer,
As freely as the streams of Eden flowed

When we were happy by them. So, depart;
Leave us to walk the remnant of our time
Out mildly in the desert. Do not seek
To harm us any more or scoff at us,
Or ere the dust be laid upon our face,
To find there the communion of the dust
And issue of the dust.—Go !

 Adam.   At once, go !

 Luc. Forgive ! and go ! Ye images of clay,
Shrunk somewhat in the mould,—what jest is this ?
What words are these to use ? By what a thought
Conceive ye of me ? Yesterday—a snake !
To-day —what ?

 Adam.   A strong spirit.

 Eve.   A sad spirit.

 Adam. Perhaps a fallen angel.—Who shall say !

 Luc. Who told thee, Adam ?

 Adam.   Thou ! The prodigy
Of thy vast brows and melancholy eyes
Which comprehend the heights of some great fall.
I think that thou hast one day worn a crown
Under the eyes of God.

 Luc.   And why of God ?

 Adam. It were no crown else. Verily, I think
Thou'rt fallen far. I had not yesterday
Said it so surely, but I know to-day
Grief by grief, sin by sin !

 Luc.   A crown, by a crown.

 Adam. Ay, mock me ! now I know more than I knew:

Now I know that thou art fallen below hope
Of final re-ascent.

   Luc.   Because?

   Adam.   Because
A spirit who expected to see God
Though at the last point of a million years,
Could dare no mockery of a ruined man
Such as this Adam.

   Luc.   Who is high and bold—
Be it said passing!—of a good red clay
Discovered on some top of Lebanon,
Or haply of Aornus, beyond sweep
Of the black eagle's wing! A furlong lower
Had made a meeker king for Eden. Soh!
Is it not possible, by sin and grief
(To give the things your names) that spirits should rise
Instead of falling?

   Adam.   Most impossible.
The Highest being the Holy and the Glad,
Whoever rises must approach delight
And sanctity in the act.

   Luc.   Ha, my clay-king!
Thou wilt not rule by wisdom very long
The after generations. Earth, methinks,
Will disinherit thy philosophy
For a new doctrine suited to thine heirs,
And class these present dogmas with the rest
Of the old-world traditions, Eden fruits
And Saurian fossils.

Eve.　　　　　　　　Speak no more with him,
Beloved! it is not good to speak with him.
Go from us, Lucifer, and speak no more!
We have no pardon which thou dost not scorn,
Nor any bliss, thou seest, for coveting,
Nor innocence for staining.　Being bereft,
We would be alone.—Go!

Luc.　　　　　　　　　　Ah! ye talk the same,
All of you—spirits and clay—go, and depart!
In Heaven they said so, and at Eden's gate,
And here, reiterant, in the wilderness.
None saith, Stay with me, for thy face is fair!
None saith, Stay with me, for thy voice is sweet!
And yet I was not fashioned out of clay.
Look on me, woman!　Am I beautiful?

Eve. Thou hast a glorious darkness.

Luc.　　　　　　　　　　　Nothing more?

Eve. I think, no more.

Luc.　　　　　False Heart—thou thinkest more!
Thou canst not choose but think, as I praise God,
Unwillingly but fully, that I stand
Most absolute in beauty.　As yourselves
Were fashioned very good at best, so *we*
Sprang very beauteous from the creant Word
Which thrilled behind us, God Himself being moved
When that august work of a perfect shape,
His dignities of sovran angel-hood,
Swept out into the universe,—divine
With thunderous movements, earnest looks of gods,

And silver-solemn clash of cymbal wings.
Whereof was I, in motion and in form,
A part not poorest. And yet,—yet, perhaps,
This beauty which I speak of, is not here,
As God's voice is not here, nor even my crown—
I do not know. What is this thought or thing
Which I call beauty? is it thought, or thing?
Is it a thought accepted for a thing?
Or both? or neither?—a pretext—a word?
Its meaning flutters in me like a flame
Under my own breath: my perceptions reel
For evermore around it, and fall off,
As if it too were holy.

    Eve.   Which it is.

    Adam. The essence of all beauty, I call love.
The attribute, the evidence, and end,
The consummation to the inward sense,
Of beauty apprehended from without,
I still call love. As form, when colourless,
Is nothing to the eye,—that pine-tree there,
Without its black and green, being all a blank,—
So, without love, is beauty undiscerned
In man or angel. Angel! rather ask
What love is in thee, what love moves to thee.
And what collateral love moves on with thee;
Then shalt thou know if thou art beautiful.

    Luc. Love! what is love? I lose it. Beauty and love
I darken to the image. Beauty—love!

                 [*He fades away, while a low music sounds.*

Adam. Thou art pale, Eve.

Eve.   The precipice of ill
Down this colossal nature, dizzies me:
And, hark! the starry harmony remote
Seems measuring the heights from whence he fell.

Adam. Think that we have not fallen so! By the hope
And aspiration, by the love and faith,
We do exceed the stature of this angel.

Eve. Happier we are than he is, by the death.

Adam. Or rather, by the life of the Lord God!
How dim the angel grows, as if that blast
Of music swept him back into the dark.

[*The music is stronger, gathering itself into uncertain articulation.*

Eve. It throbs in on us like a plaintive heart,
Pressing, with slow pulsations, vibrative,
Its gradual sweetness through the yielding air,
To such expression as the stars may use,
Most starry-sweet and strange!   With every note
That grows more loud, the angel grows more dim,
Receding in proportion to approach,
Until he stand afar,—a shade.

Adam.   Now, words.

SONG OF THE MORNING STAR TO LUCIFER.

He fades utterly away and vanishes, as it proceeds.

Mine orbèd image sinks
    Back from thee, back from thee,
As thou art fallen, methinks,
    Back from me, back from me.

O my light-bearer,
Could another fairer
Lack to thee, lack to thee?
    Ah, ah, Heosphoros!
I loved thee with the fiery love of stars
Who love by burning, and by loving move,
Too near the throned Jehovah not to love.
    Ah, ah, Heosphoros!
Their brows flash fast on me from gliding cars,
    Pale-passioned for my loss.
    Ah, ah, Heosphoros!

Mine orbèd heats drop cold
    Down from thee, down from thee,
As fell thy grace of old
    Down from me, down from me,
    O my light-bearer,
    Is another fairer
    Won to thee, won to thee?
    Ah, ah, Heosphoros,
    Great love preceded loss,
    Known to thee, known to thee.
        Ah, ah!
Thou, breathing thy communicable grace
    Of life into my light,
Mine astral faces, from thine angel face,
    Hast inly fed,
And flooded me with radiance overmuch
    From thy pure height.
        Ah, ah!   D 2

Thou, with calm, floating pinions both ways spread,
    Erect, irradiated,
    Didst sting my wheel of glory
    On, on before thee
Along the Godlight by a quickening touch!
    Ha, ha!
Around, around the firmamental ocean
I swam expanding with delirious fire!
Around, around, around, in blind desire
To be drawn upward to the Infinite—
    Ha, ha!

Until, the motion flinging out the motion
  To a keen whirl of passion and avidity,
To a dim whirl of languor and delight,
I wound in girant orbits smooth and white
    With that intense rapidity.
    Around, around,
    I wound and interwound,
While all the cyclic heavens about me spun.
Stars, planets, suns, and moons dilated broad,
Then flashed together into a single sun,
And wound, and wound in one:
And as they wound I wound,—around, around,
In a great fire I almost took for God.
    Ha, ha, Heosphoros!

    Thine angel glory sinks
    Down from me, down from me—

My beauty falls, methinks,
 Down from thee, down from thee!
  O my light-bearer,
  O my path-preparer,
 Gone from me, gone from me!
  Ah, ah, Heosphoros!
I cannot kindle underneath the brow
Of this new angel here, who is not Thou.
All things are altered since that time ago,—
And if I shine at eve, I shall not know.
  I am strange—I am slow.
  Ah, ah, Heosphoros!
Henceforward, human eyes of lovers be
The only sweetest sight that I shall see,
With tears between the looks raised up to me.
  Ah, ah!
When, having wept all night, at break of day
Above the folded hills they shall survey
My light, a little trembling, in the grey.
  Ah, ah!
And gazing on me, such shall comprehend,
 Through all my piteous pomp at morn or even
 And melancholy leaning out of heaven,
That love, their own divine, may change or end,
  That love may close in loss!
  Ah, ah, Heosphoros!

Scene.—*Farther on.   A wild open country seen vaguely in
the approaching night.*

Adam. How doth the wide and melancholy earth
Gather her hills around us, grey and ghast,
And stare with blank significance of loss
Right in our faces!   Is the wind up?
　　Eve.　　　　　　　　　　　　　Nay.
　　Adam. And yet the cedars and the junipers
Rock slowly through the mist, without a sound,
And shapes which have no certainty of shape
Drift duskly in and out between the pines,
And loom along the edges of the hills,
And lie flat, curdling in the open ground—
Shadows without a body, which contract
And lengthen as we gaze on them.
　　Eve.　　　　　　　　　　　　O life
Which is not man's nor angel's!   What is this?
　　Adam. No cause for fear.   The circle of God's life
Contains all life beside.
　　Eve.　　　　　　　　I think the earth
Is crazed with curse, and wanders from the sense
Of those first laws affixed to form and space
Or ever she knew sin.
　　Adam.　　　　　　　We will not fear:
We were brave sinning.
　　Eve.　　　　　　　　Yea, I plucked the fruit

With eyes upturned to heaven and seeing there
Our god-thrones, as the tempter said,—not GOD.
My heart, which beat then, sinks.   The sun hath sunk
Out of sight with our Eden.

  Adam.   Night is near.

  Eve. And God's curse, nearest.   Let us travel back
And stand within the sword-glare till we die,
Believing it is better to meet death
Than suffer desolation.

  Adam.   Nay, beloved!
We must not pluck death from the Maker's hand,
As erst we plucked the apple: we must wait
Until He gives death as He gave us life,
Nor murmur faintly o'er the primal gift
Because we spoilt its sweetness with our sin.

  Eve. Ah, ah! dost thou discern what I behold?

  Adam. I see all.   How the spirits in thine eyes
From their dilated orbits bound before
To meet the spectral Dread!

  Eve.   I am afraid—
Ah, ah! the twilight bristles wild with shapes
Of intermittent motion, aspect vague
And mystic bearings, which o'ercreep the earth,
Keeping slow time with horrors in the blood.
How near they reach ... and far! How grey they move—
Treading upon the darkness without feet,
And fluttering on the darkness without wings!
Some run like dogs, with noses to the ground;
Some keep one path, like sheep; some rock like trees;

Some glide like a fallen leaf; and some flow on
Copious as rivers.

    Adam.   Some spring up like fire;
And some coil . . .

    Eve.   Ah, ah! dost thou pause to say
Like what?—coil like the serpent, when he fell
From all the emerald splendour of his height
And writhed, and could not climb against the curse,
Not a ring's length.   I am afraid—afraid—
I think it is God's will to make me afraid,—
Permitting THESE to haunt us in the place
Of His belovëd angels—gone from us
Because we are not pure.   Dear Pity of God,
That didst permit the angels to go home
And live no more with us who are not pure,
Save *us* too from a loathly company—
Almost as loathly in our eyes, perhaps,
As *we* are in the purest!   Pity us—
Us too! nor shut us in the dark, away
From verity and from stability,
Or what we name such through the precedence
Of earth's adjusted uses,—leave us not
To doubt betwixt our senses and our souls,
Which are the more distraught and full of pain
And weak of apprehension!

    Adam.   Courage, Sweet!
The mystic shapes ebb back from us, and drop
With slow concentric movement, each on each,—
Expressing wider spaces,—and collapsed

In lines more definite for imagery
And clearer for relation, till the throng
Of shapeless spectra merge into a few
Distinguishable phantasms vague and grand
Which sweep out and around us vastily
And hold us in a circle and a calm.

    Eve. Strange phantasms of pale shadow! there are
        twelve.
Thou who didst name all lives, hast names for these?

    Adam. Methinks this is the zodiac of the earth,
Which rounds us with a visionary dread,
Responding with twelve shadowy signs of earth,
In fantasque apposition and approach,
To those celestial, constellated twelve
Which palpitate adown the silent nights
Under the pressure of the hand of God
Stretched wide in benediction. At this hour,
Not a star pricketh the flat gloom of heaven!
But, girdling close our nether wilderness,
The zodiac-figures of the earth loom slow,—
Drawn out, as suiteth with the place and time,
In twelve colossal shades instead of stars,
Through which the ecliptic line of mystery
Strikes bleakly with an unrelenting scope,
Foreshowing life and death.

    Eve.   By dream or sense,
Do we see this?

    Adam.   Our spirits have climbed high
By reason of the passion of our grief,

And, from the top of sense, looked over sense,
To the significance and heart of things
Rather than things themselves.

Eve.   And the dim twelve ...

Adam. Are dim exponents of the creature-life
As earth contains it.   Gaze on them, beloved!
By stricter apprehension of the sight,
Suggestions of the creatures shall assuage
The terror of the shadows,—what is known
Subduing the unknown and taming it
From all prodigious dread.   That phantasm, there,
Presents a lion, albeit twenty times
As large as any lion—with a roar
Set soundless in his vibratory jaws,
And a strange horror stirring in his mane.
And, there, a pendulous shadow seems to weigh—
Good against ill, perchance; and there, a crab
Puts coldly out its gradual shadow-claws,
Like a slow blot that spreads,—till all the ground,
Crawled over by it, seems to crawl itself.
A bull stands hornèd here with gibbous glooms;
And a ram likewise : and a scorpion writhes
Its tail in ghastly slime and stings the dark.
This way a goat leaps with wild blank of beard;
And here, fantastic fishes duskly float,
Using the calm for waters, while their fins
Throb out quick rhythms along the shallow air.
While images more human——

Eve.   How he stands,

That phantasm of a man—who is not *thou!*
Two phantasms of two men!

   Adam.   One that sustains,
And one that strives,—resuming, so, the ends
Of manhood's curse of labour.*   Dost thou see
That phantasm of a woman ?—

   Eve.   I have seen ;
But look off to those small humanities †
Which draw me tenderly across my fear,—
Lesser and fainter than my womanhood
Or yet thy manhood—with strange innocence
Set in the misty lines of head and hand.
They lean together! I would gaze on them
Longer and longer, till my watching eyes,
As the stars do in watching anything,
Should light them forward from their outline vague
To clear configuration.‥
Two spirits, of organic and inorganic nature, arise from the ground.
                        But what Shapes
Rise up between us in the open space,
And thrust me into horror, back from hope !

   Adam. Colossal Shapes—twin sovran images,
With a disconsolate, blank majesty

---

* Adam recognizes in *Aquarius*, the water-bearer, and *Sagittarius*, the archer, distinct types of the man bearing and the man combating,—the passive and active forms of human labour. I hope that the preceding zodiacal signs—transferred to the earthly shadow and representative purpose—of Aries, Taurus, Cancer, Leo, Libra, Scorpio, Capricornus, and Pisces, are sufficiently obvious to the reader.

† Her maternal instinct is excited by *Gemini*.

Set in their wondrous faces! with no look,
And yet an aspect—a significance
Of individual life and passionate ends,
Which overcomes us gazing.

                  O bleak sound,
O shadow of sound, O phantasm of thin sound!
How it comes, wheeling as the pale moth wheels,
Wheeling and wheeling in continuous wail
Around the cyclic zodiac, and gains force,
And gathers, settling coldly like a moth,
On the wan faces of these images
We see before us,—whereby modified,
It draws a straight line of articulate song
From out that spiral faintness of lament,
And, by one voice, expresses many griefs.

    First Spirit.

I am the spirit of the harmless earth.

    God spake me softly out among the stars,
As softly as a blessing of much worth;

    And then, His smile did follow unawares,
That all things fashioned so for use and duty
Might shine anointed with His chrism of beauty—

            Yet I wail!

I drave on with the worlds exultingly,

    Obliquely down the Godlight's gradual fall;
Individual aspect and complexity

    Of giratory orb and interval
Lost in the fluent motion of delight
Toward the high ends of Being beyond sight—

            Yet I wail!

Second Spirit.

I am the spirit of the harmless beasts,
    Of flying things, and creeping things, and swimming;
Of all the lives, erst set at silent feasts,
    That found the love-kiss on the goblet brimming,
And tasted in each drop within the measure
The sweetest pleasure of their Lord's good pleasure—
                    Yet I wail!
What a full hum of life around His lips
    Bore witness to the fullness of creation!
How all the grand words were full-laden ships
    Each sailing onward from enunciation
To separate existence,—and each bearing
The creature's power of joying, hoping, fearing!
                    Yet I wail!

    Eve. They wail, beloved! they speak of glory and
        God,
And they wail—wail. That burden of the song
Drops from it like its fruit, and heavily falls
Into the lap of silence.

    Adam.   Hark, again!

First Spirit.

I was so beautiful, so beautiful,
    My joy stood up within me bold to add
A word to God's,—and, when His work was full,
    To 'very good,' responded 'very glad!'
Filtered through roses, did the light enclose me,
And bunches of the grape swam blue across me—
                    Yet I wail!

Second Spirit.

I bounded with my panthers : I rejoiced
　In my young tumbling lions rolled together :
My stag, the river at his fetlocks, poised
　Then dipped his antlers through the golden weather
In the same ripple which the alligator
Left, in his joyous troubling of the water—
　　　　　Yet I wail !

First Spirit.

O my deep waters, cataract and flood,
　What wordless triumph did your voices render !
O mountain-summits, where the angels stood
　And shook from head and wing thick dews of splendour !
How, with a holy quiet, did your Earthy
Accept that Heavenly, knowing ye were worthy !
　　　　　Yet I wail !

Second Spirit.

O my wild wood-dogs, with your listening eyes !
　My horses—my ground-eagles, for swift fleeing !
My birds, with viewless wings of harmonies,
　My calm cold fishes of a silver being,
How happy were ye, living and possessing,
O fair half-souls capacious of full blessing !
　　　　　Yet I wail !

First Spirit.

I wail, I wail ! Now hear my charge to-day,
　Thou man, thou woman, marked as the misdoers
By God's sword at your backs ! I lent my clay
　To make your bodies, which had grown more flowers :

And now, in change for what I lent, ye give me
The thorn to vex, the tempest-fire to cleave me—
                    And I wail!

 Second Spirit.

I wail, I wail! Behold ye that I fasten
 My sorrow's fang upon your souls dishonoured?
Accursed transgressors! down the steep ye hasten,—
 Your crown's weight on the world, to drag it down-
   ward
Unto your ruin. Lo! my lions, scenting
The blood of wars, roar hoarse and unrelenting—
                    And I wail!

 First Spirit.

I wail, I wail! Do you hear that I wail?
 I had no part in your transgression—none.
My roses on the bough did bud not pale,
 My rivers did not loiter in the sun;
I was obedient. Wherefore in my centre
Do I thrill at this curse of death and winter?—
                    Do I wail?

 Second Spirit.

I wail, I wail! I wail in the assault
 Of undeserved perdition, sorely wounded!
My nightingale sang sweet without a fault,
 My gentle leopards innocently bounded.
We were obedient. What is this convulses
Our blameless life with pangs and fever pulses?
                    And I wail!

 Eve. I choose God's thunder and His angels' swords

To die by, Adam, rather than such words.
Let us pass out and flee.
 Adam.   We cannot flee.
This zodiac of the creatures' cruelty.
Curls round us, like a river cold and drear,
And shuts us in, constraining us to hear.
 First Spirit.
I feel your steps, O wandering sinners, strike
 A sense of death to me, and undug graves!
The heart of earth, once calm, is trembling like
 The ragged foam along the ocean-waves:
The restless earthquakes rock against each other;
The elements moan 'round me—' Mother, mother '—
   And I wail!
 Second Spirit.
Your melancholy looks do pierce me through;
 Corruption swathes the paleness of your beauty.
Why have ye done this thing?　What did we do
 That we should fall from bliss as ye from duty?
Wild shriek the hawks, in waiting for their jesses,
Fierce howl the wolves along the wildernesses—
   And I wail!
 Adam. To thee, the Spirit of the harmless earth,
To thee, the Spirit of earth's harmless lives,
Inferior creatures but still innocent,
Be salutation from a guilty mouth
Yet worthy of some audience and respect
From you who are not guilty.　If we have sinned,
God hath rebuked us, who is over us

To give rebuke or death, and if ye wail
Because of any suffering from our sin,
Ye who are under and not over us,
Be satisfied with God, if not with us,
And pass out from our presence in such peace
As we have left you, to enjoy revenge
Such as the heavens have made you.   Verily,
There must be strife between us, large as sin.

   Eve. No strife, mine Adam!   Let us not stand high
Upon the wrong we did to reach disdain,
Who rather should be humbler evermore
Since self-made sadder.   Adam! shall I speak—
I who spake once to such a bitter end—
Shall I speak humbly now, who once was proud?
I, schooled by sin to more humility
Than thou hast, O mine Adam, O my king—
My king, if not the world's?

   Adam.   Speak as thou wilt.

   Eve. Thus, then—my hand in thine—

         . . . . Sweet, dreadful Spirits!
I pray you humbly in the name of God,
Not to say of these tears, which are impure—
Grant me such pardoning grace as can go forth
From clean volitions toward a spotted will,
From the wronged to the wronger, this and no more!
I do not ask more.   I am 'ware, indeed,
That absolute pardon is impossible
From you to me, by reason of my sin,—
And that I cannot evermore, as once,

With worthy acceptation of pure joy,
Behold the trances of the holy hills
Beneath the leaning stars, or watch the vales
Dew-pallid with their morning ecstasy,—
Or hear the winds make pastoral peace between
Two grassy uplands,—and the river-wells
Work out their bubbling mysteries underground,—
And all the birds sing, till for joy of song
They lift their trembling wings as if to heave
The too-much weight of music from their heart
And float it up the æther.   I am 'ware
That these things I can no more apprehend
With a pure organ into a full delight,—
The sense of beauty and of melody
Being no more aided in me by the sense
Of personal adjustment to those heights
Of what I see well-formed or hear well-tuned,
But rather coupled darkly and made ashamed
By my percipiency of sin and fall
In melancholy of humiliant thoughts.
But, oh! fair, dreadful Spirits—albeit this
Your accusation must confront my soul,
And your pathetic utterance and full gaze
Must evermore subdue me,—be content!
Conquer me gently—as if pitying me,
Not to say loving! let my tears fall thick
As watering dews of Eden, unreproached;
And when your tongues reprove me, make me smooth,
Not ruffled—smooth and still with your reproof,

And peradventure better while more sad.
For look to it, sweet Spirits, look well to it,
It will not be amiss in you who kept
The law of your own righteousness, and keep
The right of your own griefs to mourn themselves,—
To pity me twice fallen, from that, and this,
From joy of place, and also right of wail,
'I wail' being not for me—only 'I sin.'
Look to it, O sweet Spirits!

                For was I not,
At that last sunset seen in Paradise,
When all the westering clouds flashed out in throngs
Of sudden angel-faces, face by face,
All hushed and solemn, as a thought of God
Held them suspended,—was I not, that hour,
The lady of the world, princess of life,
Mistress of feast and favour? Could I touch
A rose with my white hand, but it became
Redder at once? Could I walk leisurely
Along our swarded garden, but the grass
Tracked me with greenness? Could I stand aside
A moment underneath a cornel-tree,
But all the leaves did tremble as alive
With songs of fifty birds who were made glad
Because I stood there? Could I turn to look
With these twain eyes of mine, now weeping fast,
Now good for only weeping,—upon man,
Angel, or beast, or bird, but each rejoiced
Because I looked on him? Alas, alas!

                            E 2

And is not this much woe, to cry 'alas!'
Speaking of joy? And is not this more shame,
To have made the woe myself, from all that joy?
To have stretched my hand, and plucked it from the tree,
And chosen it for fruit? Nay, is not this
Still most despair,—to have halved that bitter fruit,
And ruined, so, the sweetest friend I have,
Turning the GREATEST to mine enemy?

    Adam. I will not hear thee speak so. Harken, Spirits!
Our God, who is the enemy of none
But only of their sin, hath set your hope
And my hope, in a promise, on this Head.
Show reverence, then, and never bruise her more
With unpermitted and extreme reproach,—
Lest, passionate in anguish, she fling down
Beneath your trampling feet, God's gift to us
Of sovranty by reason and freewill,
Sinning against the province of the Soul
To rule the soulless. Reverence her estate,
And pass out from her presence with no words!

    Eve. O dearest Heart, have patience with my heart!
O Spirits, have patience, 'stead of reverence,
And let me speak, for, not being innocent,
It little doth become me to be proud,
And I am prescient by the very hope
And promise set upon me, that henceforth
Only my gentleness shall make me great,
My humbleness exalt me. Awful Spirits,
Be witness that I stand in your reproof

But one sun's length off from my happiness—
Happy, as I have said, to look around,
Clear to look up!—And now!   I need not speak—
Ye see me what I am; ye scorn me so,
Because ye see me what I have made myself
From God's best making!   Alas,—peace foregone,
Love wronged, and virtue forfeit, and tears wept
Upon all, vainly!   Alas, me! alas,
Who have undone myself from all that best
Fairest and sweetest, to this wretchedest
Saddest and most defiled—cast out, cast down—
What word metes absolute loss? let absolute loss
Suffice you for revenge.   For *I*, who lived
Beneath the wings of angels yesterday,
Wander to-day beneath the roofless world:
I, reigning the earth's empress yesterday,
Put off from me, to-day, your hate with prayers:
I, yesterday, who answered the Lord God,
Composed and glad as singing-birds the sun,
Might shriek now from our dismal desert, 'God,'
And hear Him make reply, 'What is thy need,
Thou whom I cursed to-day?'

   Adam.   Eve!

   Eve.   *I*, at last,
Who yesterday was helpmate and delight
Unto mine Adam, am to-day the grief
And curse-mate for him.   And, so, pity us,
Ye gentle Spirits, and pardon him and me,
And let some tender peace, made of our pain,

Grow up betwixt us, as a tree might grow,
With boughs on both sides ! In the shade of which,
When presently ye shall behold us dead,—
For the poor sake of our humility,
Breathe out your pardon on our breathless lips,
And drop your twilight dews against our brows,
And stroking with mild airs our harmless hands
Left empty of all fruit, perceive your love
Distilling through your pity over us,
And suffer it, self-reconciled, to pass !

LUCIFER *rises in the circle.*

Luc. Who talks here of a complement of grief?
Of expiation wrought by loss and fall?
Of hate subduable to pity ?   Eve ?
Take counsel from thy counsellor the snake,
And boast no more in grief, nor hope from pain,
My docile Eve !   I teach you to despond,
Who taught you disobedience.   Look around ;—
Earth-spirits and phantasms hear you talk unmoved,
As if ye were red clay again and talked !
What are your words to them ? your grief to them ?
Your deaths, indeed, to them ?   Did the hand pause
For *their* sake, in the plucking of the fruit,
That they should pause for *you*, in hating you ?
Or will your grief or death, as did your sin,
Bring change upon their final doom ?   Behold,
Your grief is but your sin in the rebound,
And cannot expiate for it.

Adam.   That is true.

Luc. Ay, that is true. The clay-king testifies
To the snake's counsel,—hear him!—very true.

    Earth Spirits. I wail, I wail!

    Luc.   And certes, *that* is true.
Ye wail, ye all wail. Peradventure I
Could wail among you. O thou universe,
That holdest sin and woe,—more room for wail!

    Distant starry voice. Ah, ah, Heosphoros! Heos-
        phoros!

    Adam. Mark Lucifer! He changes awfully.

    Eve. It seems as if he looked from grief to God
And could not see Him. Wretched Lucifer!

    Adam. How he stands—yet an angel!

    Earth Spirits.   We all wail!

    Luc. (*after a pause.*) Dost thou remember, Adam,
        when the curse
Took us in Eden? On a mountain-peak
Half-sheathed in primal woods and glittering
In spasms of awful sunshine at that hour,
A lion couched, part raised upon his paws,
With his calm massive face turned full on thine,
And his mane listening. When the ended curse
Left silence in the world, right suddenly
He sprang up rampant and stood straight and stiff,
As if the new reality of death
Were dashed against his eyes, and roared so fierce,
(Such thick carnivorous passion in his throat
Tearing a passage through the wrath and fear)

And roared so wild, and smote from all the hills
Such fast keen echoes crumbling down the vales
Precipitately,—that the forest beasts,
One after one, did mutter a response
Of savage and of sorrowful complaint
Which trailed along the gorges.   Then, at once,
He fell back, and rolled crashing from the height
Into the dusk of pines.

   Adam.   It might have been.
I heard the curse alone.

   Earth Spirits.   I wail, I wail!

   Luc. That lion is the type of what I am.
And as he fixed thee with his full-faced hate,
And roared, O Adam, comprehending doom,
So, gazing on the face of the Unseen,
I cry out here between the Heavens and Earth
My conscience of this sin, this woe, this wrath,
Which damn me to this depth.

   Earth Spirits.   I wail, I wail !

   Eve. I wail—O God !

   Luc.   I scorn you that ye wail,
Who use your pretty griefs for pedestals
To stand on, beckoning pity from without,
And deal in pathos of antithesis
Of what ye *were* forsooth, and what ye are ;—
I scorn you like an angel !   Yet, one cry
I, too, would drive up like a column erect,
Marble to marble, from my heart to heaven,
A monument of anguish to transpierce

And overtop your vapoury complaints
Expressed from feeble woes.

 Earth Spirits.   I wail, I wail!

 Luc. For, O ye heavens, ye are my witnesses,
That *I*, struck out from nature in a blot,
The outcast and the mildew of things good,
The leper of angels, the excepted dust
Under the common rain of daily gifts,—
I the snake, I the tempter, I the cursed,—
To whom the highest and the lowest alike
Say, Go from us—we have no need of thee,—
Was made by God like others. Good and fair,
He did create me!—ask Him, if not fair!
Ask, if I caught not fair and silverly
His blessing for chief angels on my head
Until it grew there, a crown crystallized!
Ask, if He never called me by my name,
Lucifer—kindly said as ' Gabriel '—
Lucifer—soft as ' Michael!' while serene
I, standing in the glory of the lamps,
Answered ' my Father,' innocent of shame
And of the sense of thunder. Ha! ye think,
White angels in your niches,—I repent,
And would tread down my own offences back
To service at the footstool? *that's* read wrong!
I cry as the beast did, that I may cry—
Expansive, not appealing! Fallen so deep,
Against the sides of this prodigious pit
I cry—cry—dashing out the hands of wail

On each side, to meet anguish everywhere,
And to attest it in the ecstasy
And exaltation of a woe sustained
Because provoked and chosen.

                     Pass along
Your wilderness, vain mortals!   Puny griefs
In transitory shapes, be henceforth dwarfed
To your own conscience, by the dread extremes
Of what I am and have been.   If ye have fallen,
It is but a step's fall,—the whole ground beneath
Strewn woolly soft with promise! if ye have sinned,
Your prayers tread high as angels! if ye have grieved,
Ye are too mortal to be pitiable,
The power to die disproves the right to grieve.
Go to! ye call this ruin? I half-scorn
The ill I did you!   Were ye wronged by me,
Hated and tempted and undone of me,—
Still, what's your hurt to mine of doing hurt,
Of hating, tempting, and so ruining?
This sword's *hilt* is the sharpest, and cuts through
The hand that wields it.

                 Go! I curse you all.
Hate one another—feebly—as ye can!
I would not certes cut you short in hate,
Far be it from me! hate on as ye can!
I breathe into your faces, spirits of earth,
As wintry blast may breathe on wintry leaves
And lifting up their brownness show beneath
The branches bare.   Beseech you, spirits, give

To Eve who beggarly entreats your love
For her and Adam when they shall be dead,
An answer rather fitting to the sin
Than to the sorrow—as the heavens, I trow,
For justice' sake gave theirs.

                   I curse you both,
Adam and Eve.   Say grace as after meat,
After my curses! May your tears fall hot
On all the hissing scorns o' the creatures here,—
And yet rejoice! Increase and multiply,
Ye in your generations, in all plagues,
Corruptions, melancholies, poverties,
And hideous forms of life and fears of death,—
The thought of death being alway eminent
Immoveable and dreadful in your life,
And deafly and dumbly insignificant
Of any hope beyond,—as death itself,
Whichever of you lieth dead the first,
Shall seem to the survivor—yet rejoice!
My curse catch at you strongly, body and soul,
And HE find no redemption—nor the wing
Of seraph move your way; and yet rejoice!
Rejoice,—because ye have not, set in you,
This hate which shall pursue you—this fire-hate
Which glares without, because it burns within—·
Which kills from ashes—this potential hate,
Wherein I, angel, in antagonism
To God and his reflex beatitudes,
Moan ever in the central universe

With the great woe of striving against Love—
And gasp for space amid the Infinite,
And toss for rest amid the Desertness,
Self-orphaned by my will, and self-elect
To kingship of resistant agony
Toward the Good round me—hating good and love,
And willing to hate good and to hate love,
And willing to will on so evermore,
Scorning the past and damning the To come—
Go and rejoice! I curse you.   [LUCIFER *vanishes.*

Earth Spirits.

And we scorn you! there's no pardon
    Which can lean to you aright.
When your bodies take the guerdon
    Of the death-curse in our sight,
Then the bee that hummeth lowest shall transcend you :
    Then ye shall not move an eyelid
        Though the stars look down your eyes ;
    And the earth which ye defilëd,
        Shall expose you to the skies,—
' Lo ! these kings of ours, who sought to comprehend
        you.'

First Spirit.

And the elements shall boldly
    All your dust to dust constrain.
Unresistedly and coldly
    I will smite you with my rain.
From the slowest of my frosts is no receding.

Second Spirit.

 And my little worm, appointed
  To assume a royal part,
 He shall reign, crowned and anointed,
  O'er the noble human heart.
Give him counsel against losing of that Eden!
 Adam. Do ye scorn us? Back your scorn
  Toward your faces grey and lorn,
   As the wind drives back the rain,
  Thus I drive with passion-strife,
  I who stand beneath God's sun,
  Made like God, and, though undone,
  Not unmade for love and life.
   Lo! ye utter threats in vain.
  By my free will that chose sin,
  By mine agony within
  Round the passage of the fire,
   By the pinings which disclose
  That my native soul is higher
   Than what it chose,
We are yet too high, O Spirits, for your disdain.
 Eve. Nay, beloved! If these be low,
  We confront them from no height.
  We have stooped down to their level
  By infecting them with evil,
  And their scorn that meets our blow
   Scathes aright.
  Amen. Let it be so.

Earth Spirits.

We shall triumph—triumph greatly
   When ye lie beneath the sward.
There, our lily shall grow stately
   Though ye answer not a word,
And her fragrance shall be scornful of your silence:
   While your throne ascending calmly
     We, in heirdom of your soul,
   Flash the river, lift the palm-tree,
     The dilated ocean roll,
By the thoughts that throbbed within you, round the
     islands.

Alp and torrent shall inherit
   Your significance of will,
And the grandeur of your spirit
   Shall our broad savannahs fill;
In our winds, your exultations shall be springing.
   Even your parlance which inveigles,
     By our rudeness shall be won.
   Hearts poetic in our eagles
     Shall beat up against the sun
And strike downward in articulate clear singing.

Your bold speeches, our Behemoth
   With his thunderous jaw shall wield.
Your high fancies, shall our Mammoth
   Breathe sublimely up the shield
Of Saint Michael at God's throne, who waits to
     speed him:

Till the heavens' smooth-groovëd thunder
   Spinning back, shall leave them clear,
And the angels, smiling wonder
   With dropt looks from sphere to sphere,
Shall cry, 'Ho, ye heirs of Adam! ye exceed him.'

   Adam. Root out thine eyes, sweet, from the dreary
       ground!
Beloved, we may be overcome by God,
But not by these.

   Eve.   By God, perhaps, in these.

   Adam. I think, not so. Had God foredoomed
       despair
He had not spoken hope. He may destroy
Certes, but not deceive.

   Eve.   Behold this rose!
I plucked it in our bower of Paradise
This morning as I went forth, and my heart
Has beat against its petals all the day.
I thought it would be always red and full
As when I plucked it. *Is* it?—ye may see!
I cast it down to you that ye may see,
All of you!—count the petals lost of it,
And note the colours fainted! ye may see!
And I am as it is, who yesterday
Grew in the same place. O ye spirits of earth,
I almost, from my miserable heart,
Could here upbraid you for your cruel heart,
Which will not let me, down the slope of death,
Draw any of your pity after me,

Or lie still in the quiet of your looks,
As my flower, there, in mine.

    [*A bleak wind, quickened with indistinct human voices, spins
      around the earth-zodiac, filling the circle with its presence ;
      and then wailing off into the east, carries the rose away
      with it.* EVE *falls upon her face.* ADAM *stands erect.*

   Adam.   So, verily,
The last departs.
    Eve.   So Memory follows Hope,
And Life both.   Love said to me, 'Do not die,'
And I replied, 'O Love, I will not die.
I exiled and I will not orphan Love.'
But now it is no choice of mine to die :
My heart throbs from me.
    Adam.   Call it straightway back!
Death's consummation crowns completed life,
Or comes too early.   Hope being set on thee
For others, if for others then for thee,—
For thee and me.

    [*The wind revolves from the east, and round again to the east,
      perfumed by the Eden-rose, and full of voices which sweep
      out into articulation as they pass.*

                  Let thy soul shake its leaves
To feel the mystic wind—hark!
    Eve.   I hear life.
   Infant voices passing in the wind.
      O we live, O we live—
      And this life that we receive

Is a warm thing and a new,
Which we softly bud into
From the heart and from the brain,—
Something strange that overmuch is
   Of the sound and of the sight,
Flowing round in trickling touches,
   With a sorrow and delight,—
Yet is it all in vain?
           Rock us softly,
Lest it be all in vain.

Youthful voices passing.

O we live, O we live—
And this life that we achieve,
Is a loud thing and a bold,
Which with pulses manifold
Strikes the heart out full and fain—
Active doer, noble liver,
   Strong to struggle, sure to conquer,
Though the vessel's prow will quiver
   At the lifting of the anchor:
Yet do we strive in vain?

Infant voices passing.

           Rock us softly,
Lest it be all in vain.

Poet voices passing.

O we live, O we live—
And this life that we conceive,
Is a clear thing and a fair,
Which we set in crystal air

That its beauty may be plain!
With a breathing and a flooding
  Of the heaven-life on the whole,
While we hear the forests budding
  To the music of the soul—
Yet is it tuned in vain?

Infant voices passing.

                        Rock us softly,
  Lest it be all in vain.

Philosophic voices passing.

    O we live, O we live—
And this life that we perceive,
Is a great thing and a grave,
Which for others' use we have,
Duty-laden to remain.
We are helpers, fellow-creatures,
  Of the right against the wrong,
We are earnest-hearted teachers
  Of the truth which maketh strong—
Yet do we teach in vain?

Infant voices passing.

                        Rock us softly
  Lest it be all in vain.

Revel voices passing.

    O we live, O we live—
And this life that we reprieve,
Is a low thing and a light,
Which is jested out of sight,
And made worthy of disdain!

Strike with bold electric laughter
  The high tops of things divine—
Turn thy head, my brother, after,
  Lest thy tears fall in my wine !
For is all laughed in vain ?
Infant voices passing.
                Rock us softly,
  Lest it be all in vain.

Eve. I hear a sound of life—of life like ours—
Of laughter and of wailing, of grave speech,
Of little plaintive voices innocent,
Of life in separate courses flowing out
Like our four rivers to some outward main.
I hear life—life !

Adam.   And, so, thy cheeks have snatched
Scarlet to paleness, and thine eyes drink fast
Of glory from full cups, and thy moist lips
Seem trembling, both of them, with earnest doubts
Whether to utter words or only smile.

Eve. Shall I be mother of the coming life ?
Hear the steep generations, how they fall
Adown the visionary stairs of Time
Like supernatural thunders—far, yet near,—
Sowing their fiery echoes through the hills.
Am I a cloud to these—mother to these ?

    Earth Spirits. And bringer of the curse upon all
        these.   [EVE *sinks down again.*
    Poet voices passing.
      O we live, O we live—

And this life that we conceive,
Is a noble thing and high,
Which we climb up loftily
To view God without a stain ;
Till, recoiling where the shade is,
    We retread our steps again,
And descend the gloomy Hades
    To resume man's mortal pain.
Shall it be climbed in vain ?

Infant voices passing.

                    Rock us softly,
    Lest it be all in vain.

Love voices passing.

    O we live, O we live—
And this life we would retrieve,
Is a faithful thing apart
Which we love in, heart to heart,
Until one heart fitteth twain.
' Wilt thou be one with me ? '
' I will be one with thee.'
' Ha, ha !—we love and live ! '
Alas ! ye love and die.
Shriek—who shall reply ?
For is it not loved in vain ?

Infant voices passing.

                    Rock us softly,
    Though it be all in vain.

Aged voices passing.

    O we live, O we live—

And this life we would survive,
Is a gloomy thing and brief,
Which, consummated in grief,
Leaveth ashes for all gain.
Is it not *all* in vain?·

Infant voices passing.

Rock us softly,
Though it be *all* in vain.   [*Voices die away.*

Earth Spirits. And bringer of the curse upon all
these.

Eve. The voices of foreshown Humanity
Die off;—so let me die.

Adam.   So let us die,
When God's will soundeth the right hour of death.

Earth Spirits. And bringer of the curse upon all
these.

Eve. O Spirits! by the gentleness ye use
In winds at night, and floating clouds at noon,
In gliding waters under lily-leaves,
In chirp of crickets, and the settling hush
A bird makes in her nest with feet and wings,—
Fulfil your natures now!

Earth Spirits.   Agreed, allowed!
We gather out our natures like a cloud,
And thus fulfil their lightnings! Thus, and thus!

Harken, O harken to us!

First Spirit.

As the storm-wind blows bleakly from the norland,
As the snow-wind beats blindly on the moorland,

As the simoom drives hot across the desert,
As the thunder roars deep in the Unmeasured,
As the torrent tears the ocean-world to atoms,
As the whirlpool grinds it fathoms below fathoms,
　　　Thus,—and thus!
Second Spirit.
As the yellow toad, that spits its poison chilly,
As the tiger, in the jungle crouching stilly,
As the wild boar, with ragged tusks of anger,
As the wolf-dog, with teeth of glittering clangour,
As the vultures, that scream against the thunder,
As the owlets, that sit and moan asunder,
　　　Thus,—and thus!
Eve. Adam! God!
Adam.　　　　　　　Cruel, unrelenting Spirits!
By the power in me of the sovran soul
Whose thoughts keep pace yet with the angel's march,
I charge you into silence—trample you
Down to obedience.　I am king of you!
Earth Spirits.
　　　　Ha, ha! thou art king!
　　　　With a sin for a crown,
　　　　And a soul undone!
　　　　Thou, the antagonized,
　　　　Tortured and agonized,
　　　　Held in the ring
　　　　Of the zodiac!
　　　　Now, king, beware!
　　　　We are many and strong

Whom thou standest among,—
And we press on the air,
And we stifle thee back,
And we multiply where
Thou wouldst trample us down
From rights of our own
To an utter wrong—
And, from under the feet of thy scorn,
O forlorn,
We shall spring up like corn,
And our stubble be strong.

Adam. God, there is power in Thee! I make appeal
Unto thy kingship.

Eve.　　　　　There is pity in THEE,
O sinned against, great God!—My seed, my seed,
There is hope set on THEE—I cry to thee,
Thou mystic Seed that shalt be!—leave us not
In agony beyond what we can bear,
Fallen in debasement below thunder-mark,
A mark for scorning—taunted and perplext
By all these creatures we ruled yesterday,
Whom thou, Lord, rulest alway! O my Seed,
Through the tempestuous years that rain so thick
Betwixt my ghostly vision and thy face,
Let me have token! for my soul is bruised
Before the serpent's head is.

> [*A vision of* CHRIST *appears in the midst of the zodiac, which
> pales before the heavenly light. The Earth Spirits grow
> greyer and fainter.*

CHRIST.   I AM HERE!

Adam. This is God!—Curse us not, God, any more!

Eve. But gazing so—so—with omnific eyes,
Lift my soul upward till it touch thy feet!
Or lift it only,—not to seem too proud,—
To the low height of some good angel's feet,
For such to tread on when he walketh straight
And thy lips praise him!

CHRIST.   Spirits of the earth,
I meet you with rebuke for the reproach
And cruel and unmitigated blame
Ye cast upon your masters.   True, they have sinned;
And true their sin is reckoned into loss
For you the sinless.   Yet, your innocence,
Which of you praises? since God made your acts
Inherent in your lives, and bound your hands
With instincts and imperious sanctities
From self-defacement?   Which of you disdains
These sinners who in falling proved their height
Above you by their liberty to fall?
And which of you complains of loss by them,
For whose delight and use ye have your life
And honour in creation?   Ponder it!
This regent and sublime Humanity
Though fallen, exceeds you! this shall film your sun,
Shall hunt your lightning to its lair of cloud,
Turn back your rivers, footpath all your seas,
Lay flat your forests, master with a look
Your lion at his fasting, and fetch down

Your eagle flying. Nay, without this law
Of mandom, ye would perish,—beast by beast
Devouring,—tree by tree, with strangling roots
And trunks set tuskwise. Ye would gaze on God
With imperceptive blankness up the stars,
And mutter, 'Why, God, hast thou made us thus?'
And pining to a sallow idiocy
Stagger up blindly against the ends of life,
Then stagnate into rottenness and drop
Heavily—poor, dead matter—piecemeal down
The abysmal spaces—like a little stone
Let fall to chaos. Therefore over you
Receive man's sceptre!—therefore be content
To minister with voluntary grace
And melancholy pardon, every rite
And function in you, to the human hand!
Be ye to man as angels are to God,
Servants in pleasure, singers of delight,
Suggesters to his soul of higher things
Than any of your highest! So at last,
He shall look round on you with lids too straight
To hold the grateful tears, and thank you well,
And bless you when he prays his secret prayers,
And praise you when he sings his open songs
For the clear song-note he has learnt in you
Of purifying sweetness, and extend
Across your head his golden fantasies
Which glorify you into soul from sense.
Go, serve him for such price! That not in vain

Nor yet ignobly ye shall serve, I place
My word here for an oath, mine oath for act
To be hereafter.   In the name of which
Perfect redemption and perpetual grace,
I bless you through the hope and through the peace
Which are mine,—to the Love, which is myself.

    Eve. Speak on still, Christ! Albeit thou bless me not
In set words, I am blessed in harkening thee—
Speak, Christ!

    Christ.   Speak, Adam ! Bless the woman, man !
It is thine office.

    Adam.   Mother of the world,
Take heart before this Presence ! Lo, my voice,
Which, naming erst the creatures, did express
(God breathing through my breath) the attributes
And instincts of each creature in its name,
Floats to the same afflatus,—floats and heaves
Like a water-weed that opens to a wave,
A full-leaved prophecy affecting thee,
Out fairly and wide.   Henceforward, arise, aspire
To all the calms and magnanimities,
The lofty uses and the noble ends,
The sanctified devotion and full work,
To which thou art elect for evermore,
First woman, wife, and mother !

    Eve.   And first in sin.

    Adam. And also the sole bearer of the Seed
Whereby sin dieth. Raise the majesties
Of thy disconsolate brows, O well-beloved,

And front with level eyelids the To come,
And all the dark o' the world ! Rise, woman, rise
To thy peculiar and best altitudes
Of doing good and of enduring ill,
Of comforting for ill, and teaching good,
And reconciling all that ill and good
Unto the patience of a constant hope,—
Rise with thy daughters ! If sin came by thee,
And by sin, death,—the ransom-righteousness
The heavenly life and compensative rest
Shall come by means of thee. If woe by thee
Had issue to the world, thou shalt go forth
An angel of the woe thou didst achieve,
Found acceptable to the world instead
Of others of that name, of whose bright steps
Thy deed stripped bare the hills. Be satisfied ;
Something thou hast to bear through womanhood,
Peculiar suffering answering to the sin,—
Some pang paid down for each new human life,
Some weariness in guarding such a life,
Some coldness from the guarded, some mistrust
From those thou hast too well served, from those beloved
Too loyally some treason ; feebleness
Within thy heart, and cruelty without,
And pressures of an alien tyranny
With its dynastic reasons of larger bones
And stronger sinews. But, go to ! thy love
Shall chant itself its own beatitudes
After its own life-working. A child's kiss

Set on thy sighing lips, shall make thee glad;
A poor man served by thee, shall make thee rich,
A sick man helped by thee, shall make thee strong;
Thou shalt be served thyself by every sense
Of service which thou renderest.   Such a crown
I set upon thy head,—Christ witnessing
With looks of prompting love—to keep thee clear
Of all reproach against the sin forgone,
From all the generations which succeed.
Thy hand which plucked the apple, I clasp close,
Thy lips which spake wrong counsel, I kiss close,
I bless thee in the name of Paradise
And by the memory of Edenic joys
Forfeit and lost,—by that last cypress tree
Green at the gate, which thrilled as we came out,
And by the blessed nightingale which threw
Its melancholy music after us,—
And by the flowers, whose spirits full of smells
Did follow softly, plucking us behind
Back to the gradual banks and vernal bowers
And fourfold river-courses.—By all these,
I bless thee to the contraries of these,
I bless thee to the desert and the thorns,
To the elemental change and turbulence,
And to the roar of the estranged beasts,
And to the solemn dignities of grief,—
To each one of these ends,—and to their END
Of Death and the hereafter.

   Eve.   I accept

For me and for my daughters this high part
Which lowly shall be counted.   Noble work
Shall hold me in the place of garden-rest,
And in the place of Eden's lost delight
Worthy endurance of permitted pain;
While on my longest patience there shall wait
Death's speechless angel, smiling in the east
Whence cometh the cold wind.   I bow myself
Humbly henceforward on the ill I did,
That humbleness may keep it in the shade.
Shall it be so? shall I smile, saying so?
O Seed! O King! O God, who *shalt* be seed,—
What shall I say?   As Eden's fountains swelled
Brightly betwixt their banks, so swells my soul
Betwixt thy love and power!

                       And, sweetest thoughts
Of foregone Eden! now, for the first time
Since God said 'Adam,' walking through the trees,
I dare to pluck you as I plucked erewhile
The lily or pink, the rose or heliotrope.
So pluck I you—so largely—with both hands,
And throw you forward on the outer earth
Wherein we are cast out, to sweeten it.

   Adam. As thou, Christ, to illume it, holdest Heaven
Broadly over our heads.

      [*The* CHRIST *is gradually transfigured during the following
        phrases of dialogue, into humanity and suffering.*

   Eve.   O Saviour Christ.

Thou standest mute in glory, like the sun!

    Adam. We worship iu Thy silence, Saviour Christ!

    Eve. Thy brows grow grander with a forecast woe,—
Diviner, with the possible of death.
We worship in Thy sorrow, Saviour Christ!

    Adam. How do Thy clear, still eyes transpierce our
        souls,
As gazing *through* them toward the Father-throne
In a pathetical, full Deity,
Serenely as the stars gaze through the air
Straight on each other!

    Eve.   O pathetic Christ,
Thou standest mute in glory, like the moon!

    Christ. Eternity stands alway fronting God;
A stern colossal image, with blind eyes
And grand dim lips that murmur evermore
God, God, God! while the rush of life and death,
The roar of act and thought, of evil and good,
The avalanches of the ruining worlds
Tolling down space,—the new worlds' genesis
Budding in fire,—the gradual humming growth
Of the ancient atoms and first forms of earth,
The slow procession of the swathing seas
And firmamental waters,—and the noise
Of the broad, fluent strata of pure airs,—
All these flow onward in the intervals
Of that reiterated sound of—God!
Which word, innumerous angels straightway lift
Wide on celestial altitudes of song

And choral adoration, and then drop
The burden softly, shutting the last notes
In silver wings.   Howbeit in the noon of time
Eternity shall wax as dumb as Death,
While a new voice beneath the spheres shall cry,
' God! why hast thou forsaken me, my God?'
And not a voice in Heaven shall answer it.

[*The transfiguration is complete in sadness.*

Adam. Thy speech is of the Heavenlies, yet, O Christ,
Awfully human are thy voice and face!
Eve. My nature overcomes me from thine eyes.
CHRIST. In the set noon of time, shall one from
         Heaven,
An angel fresh from looking upon God,
Descend before a woman, blessing her
With perfect benediction of pure love,
For all the world in all its elements,
For all the creatures of earth, air, and sea,
For all men in the body and in the soul,
Unto all ends of glory and sanctity.
Eve. O pale, pathetic Christ—I worship thee!
I thank thee for that woman!
      CHRIST.   ·   Then, at last,
I, wrapping round me your humanity,
Which being sustained, shall neither break nor burn
Beneath the fire of Godhead, will tread earth.
And ransom you and it, and set strong peace
Betwixt you and its creatures.   With my pangs

I will confront your sins; and since those sins
Have sunken to all Nature's heart from yours,
The tears of my clean soul shall follow them
And set a holy passion to work clear
Absolute consecration.   In my brow
Of kingly whiteness, shall be crowned anew
Your discrowned human nature.   Look on me!
As I shall be uplifted on a cross
In darkness of eclipse and anguish dread,
So shall I lift up in my piercëd hands,
Not into dark, but light—not unto death,
But life,—beyond the reach of guilt and grief,
The whole creation.   Henceforth in my name
Take courage, O thou woman,—man, take hope!
Your grave shall be as smooth as Eden's sward,
Beneath the steps of your prospective thoughts,
And, one step past it, a new Eden-gate
Shall open on a hinge of harmony
And let you through to mercy.   Ye shall fall
No more, within that Eden, nor pass out
Any more from it.   In which hope, move on,
First sinners and first mourners!   Live and love,—
Doing both nobly, because lowlily!
Live and work, strongly, because patiently!
And, for the deed of death, trust it to God
That it be well done, unrepented of,
And not to loss!   And thence, with constant prayers
Fasten your souls so high, that constantly
The smile of your heroic cheer may float

Above all floods of earthly agonies,
Purification being the joy of pain !

[*The vision of* CHRIST *vanishes.* ADAM *and* EVE *stand in an
ecstasy. The earth-zodiac pales away shade by shade, as
the stars, star by star, shine out in the sky; and the following chant from the two* Earth Spirits *(as they sweep
back into the zodiac and disappear with it) accompanies
the process of change.*

Earth Spirits.

By the mighty word thus spoken
    Both for living and for dying,
We our homage-oath, once broken,
    Fasten back again in sighing,
And the creatures and the elements renew their cove-
nanting.

Here, forgive us all our scorning;
    Here, we promise milder duty :
And the evening and the morning
    Shall re-organize in beauty
A sabbath day of sabbath joy, for universal chanting.

And if, still, this melancholy
    May be strong to overcome us,
If this mortal and unholy
    We still fail to cast out from us,
If we turn upon you, unaware, your own dark in-
fluences,—

If ye tremble when surrounded
   By our forest pine and palm-trees,
If we cannot cure the wounded
   With our gum-trees and our balm-trees,
And if your souls all mournfully sit down among your
   senses,—

Yet, O mortals, do not fear us !
   We are gentle in our languor ;
Much more good ye shall have near us
   Than any pain or anger,
And our God's refracted blessing in our blessing shall
   be given.

By the desert's endless vigil
   We will solemnize your passions,
By the wheel of the black eagle
   We will teach you exaltations,
When he sails against the wind, to the white spot up
   in heaven.

Ye shall find us tender nurses
   To your weariness of nature,
And our hands shall stroke the curse's
   Dreary furrows from the creature,
Till your bodies shall lie smooth in death and straight
   and slumberful.

Then, a couch we will provide you
   Where no summer heats shall dazzle,

Strewing on you and beside you
Thyme and rosemary and basil,
And the yew-tree shall grow overhead to keep all safe
and cool.

Till the Holy blood awaited
Shall be chrism around us running,
Whereby, newly-consecrated
We shall leap up in God's sunning,
To join the spheric company which purer worlds as-
semble :

While, renewed by new evangels,
Soul-consummated, made glorious,
Ye shall brighten past the angels,
Ye shall kneel to Christ victorious,
And the rays around his feet beneath your sobbing
lips shall tremble.

[*The phantastic vision has all passed ; the earth-zodiac has
broken like a belt, and is dissolved from the desert. The
Earth Spirits vanish, and the stars shine out above.*

CHORUS OF INVISIBLE ANGELS,

While ADAM *and* EVE *advance into the desert, hand in hand.*

Hear our heavenly promise
Through your mortal passion!
Love, ye shall have from us,
In a pure relation.

As a fish or bird
  Swims or flies, if moving,
We unseen are heard
  To live on by loving.
Far above the glances
  Of your eager eyes,
    Listen! we are loving.
Listen, through man's ignorances,
Listen, through God's mysteries,
Listen down the heart of things,—
Ye shall hear our mystic wings

  Murmurous with loving.
  Through the opal door
  Listen evermore
  How we live by loving!

First semichorus.

When your bodies therefore
  Reach the grave their goal,
Softly will we care for
  Each enfranchised soul.
Softly and unlothly
  Through the door of opal
  Toward the heavenly people,
Floated on a minor fine
Into the full chant divine,
  We will draw you smoothly,—
While the human in the minor
Makes the harmony diviner.
    Listen to our loving!

Second semichorus.

 There, a sough of glory
  Shall breathe on you as you come,
 Ruffling round the doorway
  All the light of angeldom.
 From the empyrean centre
  Heavenly voices shall repeat,
 'Souls redeemed and pardoned, enter,
  For the chrism on you is sweet!'
 And every angel in the place
 Lowlily shall bow his face,
  Folded fair on softened sounds,
 Because upon your hands and feet
  He images his Master's wounds.
   Listen to our loving!

First semichorus.

 So, in the universe's
  Consummated undoing,
 Our seraphs of white mercies
  Shall hover round the ruin.
 Their wings shall stream upon the flame
 As if incorporate of the same
  In elemental fusion;
 And calm their faces shall burn out
 With a pale and mastering thought,
 And a steadfast looking of desire
 From out between the clefts of fire,—
 While they cry, in the Holy's name,

> To the final Restitution.
> Listen to our loving!

Second semichorus.

> So, when the day of God is
> To the thick graves accompted,
> Awaking the dead bodies
> The angel of the trumpet
> Shall split and shatter the earth
> To the roots of the grave
> Which never before were slackened,
> And quicken the charnel birth
> With his blast so clear and brave
> That the Dead shall start and stand erect,
> And every face of the burial-place
> Shall the awful, single look reflect
> Wherewith he them awakened.
> Listen to our loving!

First semichorus.

> But wild is the horse of Death.
> He will leap up wild at the clamour
> Above and beneath.
> And where is his Tamer
> On that last day,
> When he crieth, Ha, ha!
> To the trumpet's blare,
> And paweth the earth's Aceldama?
> When he tosseth his head,
> The drear-white steed,
> And ghastlily champeth the last moon-ray—

What angel there
Can lead him away,
That the living may rule for the Dead

Second semichorus.

Yet a TAMER shall be found!
One more bright than seraph crowned,
And more strong than cherub bold,
Elder, too, than angel old,
By his grey eternities.
He shall master and surprise
The steed of Death.
For He is strong, and He is fain.
He shall quell him with a breath,
And shall lead him where He will,
With a whisper in the ear,
Full of fear,
And a hand upon the mane,
Grand and still.

First semichorus.

Through the flats of Hades where the souls assemble
He will guide the Death-steed calm between their
ranks,
While, like beaten dogs, they a little moan and tremble
To see the darkness curdle from the horse's glittering
flanks.
Through the flats of Hades where the dreary shade is,
Up the steep of heaven will the Tamer guide the
steed,—
Up the spheric circles, circle above circle,

We who count the ages, shall count the tolling tread—
Every hoof-fall striking a blinder, blanker sparkle
From the stony orbs, which shall show as they were
    dead.
   Second semichorus.

All the way the Death-steed with tolling hoofs shall
    travel,
Ashen grey the planets shall be motionless as stones,
Loosely shall the systems eject their parts coæval,
Stagnant in the spaces shall float the pallid moons :
Suns that touch their apogees, reeling from their level,
Shall run back on their axles, in wild, low broken tunes.
   Chorus.

Up against the arches of the crystal ceiling,
From the horse's nostrils shall steam the blurting
    breath :
Up between the angels pale with silent feeling,
Will the Tamer calmly lead the horse of Death.
   Semichorus.

Cleaving all that silence, cleaving all that glory,
Will the Tamer lead him straightway to the Throne ;
' Look out, O Jehovah, to this I bring before Thee,
With a hand nail-piercëd, I who am thy Son.'
Then the Eye Divinest, from the Deepest, flaming,
On the mystic courser shall look out in fire :
Blind the beast shall stagger where It overcame him,
Meek as lamb at pasture, bloodless in desire.
Down the beast shall shiver,—slain amid the taming,—
And, by Life essential, the phantasm Death expire.

Chorus.

> Listen, man, through life and death,
> Through the dust and through the breath,
>> Listen down the heart of things!
>> Ye shall hear our mystic wings
>> Murmurous with loving.

A Voice from below. Gabriel, thou Gabriel!

A Voice from above. What wouldst *thou* with me?

First Voice. I heard thy voice sound in the angels' song
And I would give thee question.

Second Voice. Question me!

First Voice. Why have I called thrice to my Morning
> Star

And had no answer? All the stars are out,
And answer in their places. Only in vain
I cast my voice against the outer rays
Of *my* Star shut in light behind the sun.
No more reply than from a breaking string,
Breaking when touched. Or is she *not* my star?
Where *is* my Star—my Star? Have ye cast down
Her glory like my glory? has she waxed
Mortal, like Adam? has she learnt to hate
Like any angel?

Second Voice. She is sad for thee.
All things grow sadder to thee, one by one.

Angel chorus.

> Live, work on, O Earthy!
> By the Actual's tension,

Speed the arrow worthy
  Of a pure ascension!
From the low earth round you,
  Reach the heights above you:
From the stripes that wound you,
  Seek the loves that love you!
God's divinest burneth plain
Through the crystal diaphane
  Of our loves that love you.

First Voice. Gabriel, O Gabriel!

Second Voice. What wouldst *thou* with me?

First Voice. Is it true, O thou Gabriel, that the crown
Of sorrow which I claimed, another claims?
That HE claims THAT too?

Second Voice.   Lost one, it is true.

First Voice. That HE will be an exile from his
        heaven,
To lead those exiles homeward?

Second Voice.   It is true.

First Voice. That HE will be an exile by his will,
As I by mine election?

Second Voice.   It is true.

First Voice. That *I* shall stand sole exile finally,—
Made desolate for fruition?

Second Voice.   It is true.

First Voice. Gabriel!

Second Voice.   I hearken.

First Voice.   Is it true besides—
Aright true—that mine orient Star will give

Her name of 'Bright and Morning-Star' to HIM,—
And take the fairness of his virtue back
To cover loss and sadness ?

  Second Voice.   It is true.

  First Voice. UNTRUE. UNTRUE! O Morning-Star, O
    MINE,
Who sittest secret in a veil of light
Far up the starry spaces, say—*Untrue!*
Speak but so loud as doth a wasted moon
To Tyrrhene waters. I am Lucifer.

      [*A pause. Silence in the stars*
All things grow sadder to me, one by one.

 Angel chorus.
    Exiled human creatures,
     Let your hope grow larger
    Larger grows the vision
     Of the new delight.
    From this chain of Nature's
     God is the Discharger,
    And the Actual's prison
     Opens to your sight.
 Semichorus.
    Calm the stars and golden
     In a light exceeding :
    What their rays have measured
     Let your feet fulfil !
    These are stars beholden
     By your eyes in Eden,

Yet, across the desert,
   See them shining still!

Chorus.

Future joy and far light
   Working such relations.
Hear us singing gently
   Exiled is not lost !
God, above the starlight,
   God, above the patience,
Shall at last present ye
   Guerdons worth the cost.
Patiently enduring,
   Painfully surrounded,
Listen how we love you,
   Hope the uttermost !
Waiting for that curing
   Which exalts the wounded,
Hear us sing above you—
   EXILED, BUT NOT LOST !

[*The stars shine on brightly while* ADAM *and* EVE *pursue their
way into the far wilderness. There is a sound through the
silence, as of the falling tears of an angel.*

THE SERAPHIM.

I look for Angels' songs, and hear Him cry.
GILES FLETCHER.

THE SERAPHIM.

—◆—

PART THE FIRST.

[*It is the time of the Crucifixion ; and the angels of heaven have departed towards the earth, except the two* seraphim, ADOR *the Strong and* ZERAH *the Bright One.*
The place is the outer side of the shut heavenly gate.]

Ador. O SERAPH, pause no more!
Beside this gate of heaven we stand alone.
  Zerah. Of heaven!
  Ador.   Our brother hosts are gone—
  Zerah. Are gone before.
  Ador. And the golden harps the angels bore
      To help the songs of their desire,
      Still burning from their hands of fire,
      Lie without touch or tone
        Upon the glass-sea shore.
  Zerah. Silent upon the glass-sea shore!
  Ador. There the Shadow from the throne
      Formless with infinity
      Hovers o'er the crystal sea

Awfuller than light derived,
   And red with those primæval heats
     Whereby all life has lived.
Zerah. Our visible God, our heavenly seats!
Ador. Beneath us sinks the pomp angelical,
   Cherub and seraph, powers and virtues, all,—
     The roar of whose descent has died
  To a still sound, as thunder into rain.
     Immeasurable space spreads magnified
  With that thick life, along the plane
  The worlds slid out on.   What a fall
     And eddy of wings innumerous, crossed
     By trailing curls that have not lost
     The glitter of the God-smile shed
     On every prostrate angel's head!
     What gleaming up of hands that fling
     Their homage in retorted rays,
     From high instinct of worshipping,
       And habitude of praise!
Zerah. Rapidly they drop below us.
     Pointed palm and wing and hair
     Indistinguishable show us
     Only pulses in the air
     Throbbing with a fiery beat,
     As if a new creation heard
     Some divine and plastic word,
  And trembling at its new-found being,
    Awakened at our feet.
Ador. Zerah, do not wait for seeing!

His voice, his, that thrills us so
As we our harpstrings, uttered *Go,*
Behold the Holy in his woe!
And all are gone, save thee and—

Zerah.   Thee!

Ador. I stood the nearest to the throne
In hierarchical degree,
What time the Voice said *Go!*
And whether I was moved alone
By the storm-pathos of the tone
Which swept through heaven the alien name of *woe,*
Or whether the subtle glory broke
Through my strong and shielding wings,
Bearing to my finite essence
Incapacious of their presence,
Infinite imaginings,
None knoweth save the Throned who spoke;
But I who at creation stood upright
And heard the God-breath move
Shaping the words that lightened, ' Be there light,'
Nor trembled but with love,
Now fell down shudderingly,
My face upon the pavement whence I had towered,
As if in mine immortal overpowered
By God's eternity.

Zerah. Let me wait!—let me wait!—

Ador. Nay, gaze not backward through the gate!
God fills our heaven with God's own solitude
Till all the pavements glow.

His Godhead being no more subdued
    By itself, to glories low
      Which seraphs can sustain,
    What if thou, in gazing so,
    Shouldst behold but only one
    Attribute, the veil undone—
Even that to which we dare to press
    Nearest, for its gentleness—
      Ay, his love!
    How the deep ecstatic pain
    Thy being's strength would capture!
    Without language for the rapture,
    Without music strong to come
      And set the adoration free,
    For ever, ever, wouldst thou be
    Amid the general chorus dumb,
God-stricken to seraphic agony.
    Or, brother, what if on thine eyes
      In vision bare should rise
The life-fount whence his hand did gather
      With solitary force
      Our immortalities!
Straightway how thine own would wither,
    Falter like a human breath,
    And shrink into a point like death,
      By gazing on its source!—
      My words have imaged dread.
    Meekly hast thou bent thine head,
    And dropt thy wings in languishment

Overclouding foot and face,
    As if God's throne were eminent
      Before thee, in the place.
      Yet not—not so,
O loving spirit and meek, dost thou fulfil
The supreme Will.
Not for obeisance but obedience,
Give motion to thy wings! Depart from hence!
      The voice said ' Go!
   Zerah Beloved, I depart.
His will is as a spirit within my spirit,
A portion of the being I inherit.
His will is mine obedience. I resemble
A flame all undefilëd though it tremble;
I go and tremble. Love me, O beloved!
      O thou, who stronger art,
And standest ever near the Infinite,
      Pale with the light of Light,
Love me, beloved! me, more newly made,
      More feeble, more afraid;
And let me hear with mine thy pinions moved,
As close and gentle as the loving are,
That love being near, heaven may not seem so far.
   Ador. I am near thee and I love thee.
      Were I loveless, from thee gone,
      Love is round, beneath, above thee,
      God, the omnipresent one.
      Spread the wing, and lift the brow!
      Well-beloved, what fearest thou?

Zerah. I fear, I fear—

Ador.   What fear?

Zerah.   The fear of earth.

Ador. Of earth, the God-created and God-praised
In the hour of birth?
Where every night the moon in light
Doth lead the waters silver-faced?
    Where every day the sun doth lay
A rapture to the heart of all
The leafy and reeded pastoral,
As if the joyous shout which burst
From angel lips to see him first,
    Had left a silent echo in his ray?
    Zerah. Of earth—the God-created and God-curst,
        Where man is, and the thorn.
        Where sun and moon have borne
        No light to souls forlorn.
Where Eden's tree of life no more uprears
    Its spiral leaves and fruitage, but instead
    The yew-tree bows its melancholy head
And all the undergrasses kills and seres.
    Ador. Of earth the weak,
Made and unmade?
Where men that faint, do strive for crowns that fade?
Where, having won the profit which they seek,
They lie beside the sceptre and the gold
With fleshless hands that cannot wield or hold,
And the stars shine in their unwinking eyes?
    Zerah. Of earth the bold,

Where the blind matter wrings
An awful potence out of impotence,
Bowing the spiritual things
    To the things of sense.
Where the human will replies
With ay and no,
Because the human pulse is quick or slow.
Where Love succumbs to Change,
With only his own memories, for revenge.
And the fearful mystery—

    Ador.   called Death ?

    Zerah. Nay, death is fearful,—but who saith
     ' To die,' is comprehensible.
      What's fearfuller, thou knowest well,
      Though the utterance be not for thee,
      Lest it blanch thy lips from glory—
      Ay! the cursed thing that moved
      A shadow of ill, long time ago,
      Across our heaven's own shining floor,
      And when it vanished, some who were
      On thrones of holy empire there,
      Did reign—were seen—were—never more.
        Come nearer, O beloved !

    Ador. I am near thee.   Didst thou bear thee
     Ever to this earth ?

    Zerah.   Before.
      When thrilling from His hand along
      Its lustrous path with spheric song
      The earth was deathless, sorrowless.

Unfearing, then, pure feet might press
The grasses brightening with their feet,
For God's own voice did mix its sound
In a solemn confluence oft
With the rivers' flowing round,
And the life-tree's waving soft.
Beautiful new earth and strange!

Ador. Hast thou seen it since—the change?

Zerah. Nay, or wherefore should I fear
  To look upon it now?
I have beheld the ruined things
Only in depicturings
Of angels from an earthly mission,—
Strong one, even upon thy brow,
When, with task completed, given
Back to us in that transition,
I have beheld thee silent stand,
Abstracted in the seraph band,
  Without a smile in heaven.

Ador. Then thou wast not one of those
Whom the loving Father chose
In visionary pomp to sweep
O'er Judæa's grassy places,
O'er the shepherds and the sheep,
Though thou art so tender?—dimming,
All the stars except one star
With their brighter kinder faces.
And using heaven's own tune in hymning,
While deep response from earth's own mountains ran,

'Peace upon earth, goodwill to man.'

Zerah. 'Glory to God.' I said amen afar.
And those who from that earthly mission are,
 Within mine ears have told
That the seven everlasting Spirits did hold
With such a sweet and prodigal constraint
The meaning yet the mystery of the song
What time they sang it, on their natures strong,
That, gazing down on earth's dark steadfastness
And speaking the new peace in promises,
The love and pity made their voices faint
Into the low and tender music, keeping
The place in heaven of what on earth is weeping.

Ador. Peace upon earth. Come down to it.

Zerah.   Ah me !
I hear thereof uncomprehendingly.
Peace where the tempest, where the sighing is,
And worship of the idol, 'stead of His ?

Ador. Yea, peace, where He is.

Zerah.   He !
Say it again.

Ador.   Where He is.

Zerah.   Can it be
That earth retains a tree
Whose leaves, like Eden foliage can be swayed
By the breathing of His voice, nor shrink and fade ?

Ador. There is a tree !—it hath no leaf nor root ;
Upon it hangs a curse for all its fruit :
 Its shadow on His head is laid.

  For He, the crownëd Son,
  Has left his crown and throne,
  Walks earth in Adam's clay,
  Eve's snake to bruise and slay—
Zerah. Walks earth in clay?
Ador. And walking in the clay which he created,
  He through it shall touch death.
What do I utter? what conceive? did breath
Of demon howl it in a blasphemy?
Or was it mine own voice, informed, dilated
By the seven confluent Spirits?—Speak—answer me!
Who said man's victim was his deity?
  Zerah. Beloved, beloved, the word came forth from
   thee.
Thine eyes are rolling a tempestuous light
  Above, below, around,
As putting thunder-questions without cloud,
  Reverberate without sound,
To universal nature's depth and height.
The tremor of an inexpressive thought
Too self-amazed to shape itself aloud,
O'erruns the awful curving of thy lips;
  And while thine hands are stretched above,
   As newly they had caught
Some lightning from the Throne, or showed the Lord
  Some retributive sword,
Thy brows do alternate with wild eclipse
And radiance, with contrasted wrath and love,
  As God had called thee to a seraph's part,

With a man's quailing heart.
   Ador. O heart—O heart of man!
     O ta'en from human clay
To be no seraph's but Jehovah's own!
     Made holy in the taking,
     And yet unseparate
    From death's perpetual ban,
And human feelings sad and passionate:
Still subject to the treacherous forsaking
Of other hearts, and its own steadfast pain.
O heart of man—of God! which God has ta'en
From out the dust, with its humanity
Mournful and weak yet innocent around it,
And bade its many pulses beating lie
Beside that incommunicable stir
Of Deity wherewith He interwound it.
O man! and is thy nature so defiled
That all that holy Heart's devout law-keeping,
And low pathetic beat in deserts wild,
And gushings pitiful of tender weeping
For traitors who consigned it to such woe—
That all could cleanse thee not, without the flow
Of blood, the life-blood—*His*—and streaming *so?*
O earth the thundercleft, windshaken, where
The louder voice of ' blood and blood' doth rise,
Hast thou an altar for this sacrifice?
    O heaven! O vacant throne!
O crownèd hierarchies that wear your crown
    When His is put away!

Are ye unshaméd that ye cannot dim
Your alien brightness to be liker him,
Assume a human passion, and down-lay
Your sweet secureness for congenial fears,
And teach your cloudless ever-burning eyes
     The mystery of his tears?

  Zerah. I am strong, I am strong.
    Were I never to see my heaven again,
    I would wheel to earth like the tempest rain
    Which sweeps there with an exultant sound.
    To lose its life as it reaches the ground.
    I am strong, I am strong.
    Away from mine inward vision swim
    The shining seats of my heavenly birth,
    I see but his, I see but him—
    The Maker's steps on his cruel earth.
    Will the bitter herbs of earth grow sweet
    To me, as trodden by his feet?
    Will the vexed, accurst humanity,
    As worn by him, begin to be
    A blessed, yea, a sacred thing
    For love and awe and ministering?
      I am strong, I am strong.
    By our angel ken shall we survey
    His loving smile through his woeful clay?
      I am swift, I am strong,
    The love is bearing me along.
  Ador. One love is bearing us along.

PART THE SECOND.

[*Mid-air, above Judæa.* ADOR *and* ZERAH *are a little apart from the visible* angelic hosts.]

Ador. BELOVED! dost thou see ?—
Zerah.　　　Thee,—thee.
　Thy burning eyes already are
　Grown wild and mournful as a star
　Whose occupation is for aye
　To look upon the place of clay
　　Whereon thou lookest now.
　The crown is fainting on thy brow
　To the likeness of a cloud,
　The forehead's self a little bowed
　From its aspect high and holy,
　As it would in meekness meet
　Some seraphic melancholy :
　Thy very wings that lately flung
　An outline clear, do flicker here
　And wear to each a shadow hung,
　　Dropped across thy feet.
　In these strange contrasting glooms
　Stagnant with the scent of tombs,
　Seraph faces, O my brother,
　Show awfully to one another.

Ador. Dost thou see?

Zerah.   Even so; I see
   Our empyreal company,
    Alone the memory of their brightness
    Left in them, as in thee.
The circle upon circle, tier on tier,
    Piling earth's hemisphere
    With heavenly infiniteness,
    Above us and around,
Straining the whole horizon like a bow:
Their songful lips divorcèd from all sound,
A darkness gliding down their silvery glances,—
Bowing their steadfast solemn countenances
As if they heard God speak, and could not glow.
   Ador. Look downward! dost thou see?
   Zerah. And wouldst thou press *that* vision on my
     words?
Doth not earth speak enough
Of change and of undoing,
Without a seraph's witness?   Oceans rough
With tempest, pastoral swards
Displaced by fiery deserts, mountains ruing
The bolt fallen yesterday,
That shake their piny heads, as who would say
' We are too beautiful for our decay '—
Shall seraphs speak of these things?   Let alone
   Earth to her earthly moan!
   Voice of all things. Is there no moan but hers?
   Ador. Hearest thou the attestation

Of the rousēd universe
Like a desert lion shaking
Dews of silence from its mane ?
With an irrepressive passion
    Uprising at once,
Rising up and forsaking
Its solemn state in the circle of suns,
    To attest the pain
Of him who stands (O patience sweet !)
In his own hand-prints of creation,
   With human feet ?

Voice of all things. Is there no moan but ours ?

Zerah. Forms, Spaces, Motions wide,
  O meek, insensate things,
O congregated matters ! who inherit
  Instead of vital powers,
  Impulsions God-supplied ;
  Instead of influent spirit,
  A clear informing beauty ;
  Instead of creature-duty,
  Submission calm as rest.
  Lights, without feet or wings,
  In golden courses sliding !
  Glooms, stagnantly subsiding,
Whose lustrous heart away was prest
    Into the argent stars !
  Ye crystal, firmamental bars
  That hold the skyey waters free
  From tide or tempest's ecstasy !

Airs universal! thunders lorn
That wait your lightnings in cloud-cave
Hewn out by the winds!   O brave
And subtle elements! the Holy
Hath charged me by your voice with folly.*
Enough, the mystic arrow leaves its wound.
Return ye to your silences inborn,
Or to your inarticulated sound!

   Ador. Zerah!

   Zerah. Wilt *thou* rebuke?
God hath rebuked me, brother.   I am weak.

   Ador. Zerah, my brother Zerah! could I speak
Of thee, 'twould be of love to thee.

   Zerah.   Thy look
Is fixed on earth, as mine upon thy face.
Where shall I seek His?

                   I have thrown
One look upon earth, but one,
Over the blue mountain-lines,
Over the forests of palms and pines.
Over the harvest-lands golden,
Over the valleys that fold in
The gardens and vines—
   He is not there.
All these are unworthy
Those footsteps to bear,
   Before which, bowing down
I would fain quench the stars of my crown

* " His angels He charged with folly."—*Job* iv. 18.

In the dark of the earthy.
Where shall I seek him ?

No reply ?

Hath language left thy lips, to place
Its vocal in thine eye ?
Ador, Ador ! are we come
To a double portent, that
Dumb matter grows articulate
And songful seraphs dumb ?
Ador, Ador !

Ador. I constrain
The passion of my silence. None
Of those places gazed upon
Are gloomy enow to fit his pain.
Unto him, whose forming word
Gave to Nature flower and sward,
She hath given back again,
For the myrtle, the thorn,
For the sylvan calm, the human scorn.
Still, still, reluctant seraph, gaze beneath !
There is a city——

Zerah. Temple and tower,
Palace and purple would droop like a flower,
(Or a cloud at our breath)
If he neared in his state
The outermost gate.

Ador. Ah me, not so
In the state of a king did the victim go !
And THOU who hangest mute of speech

'Twixt heaven and earth, with forehead yet
Stainëd by the bloody sweat,
God! man! Thou hast forgone thy throne in each.
Zerah. Thine eyes behold him?
Ador.   Yea, below.

Track the gazing of mine eyes,
Naming God within thine heart
That its weakness may depart
    And the vision rise!
Seest thou yet, beloved?
Zerah.   I see

Beyond the city, crosses three
And mortals three that hang thereon
'Ghast and silent to the sun.
Round them blacken and welter and press
Staring multitudes whose father
Adam was, whose brows are dark
With his Cain's corroded mark,—
Who curse with looks. Nay—let me rather
Turn unto the wilderness!
Ador. Turn not! God dwells with men.
Zerah.   Above
He dwells with angels, and they love.
Can these love? With the living's pride
They stare at those who die, who hang
In their sight and die. They bear the streak
Of the crosses' shadow, black not wide,
To fall on their heads, as it swerves aside
    When the victims' pang

Makes the dry wood creak.

Ador. The cross—the cross!

Zerah.   A woman kneels

The mid cross under,

With white lips asunder,

And motion on each.

They throb, as she feels,

With a spasm, not a speech ;

And her lids, close as sleep,

Are less calm, for the eyes

Have made room there to weep

Drop on drop—

Ador.   Weep? Weep blood,

All women, all men !

He sweated it, he,

For your pale womanhood

And base manhood.   Agree

That these water-tears, then,

Are vain, mocking like laughter.

Weep blood !   Shall the flood

Of salt curses, whose foam is the darkness, on roll

Forward, on from the strand of the storm-beaten
     years,

And back from the rocks of the horrid hereafter,

And up, in a coil, from the present's wrath-spring,

Yea, down from the windows of heaven opening,

Deep calling to deep as they meet on His soul—

        And men weep only tears ?

Zerah. Little drops in the lapse !

And yet, Ador, perhaps
It is all that they can.
Tears! the lovingest man
Has no better bestowed
Upon man.

Ador.　　　　　　Nor on God.

Zerah.　　　　　　Do all-givers need gifts?
If the Giver said ' Give,' the first motion would slay
Our Immortals, the echo would ruin away
The same worlds which he made.　Why, what angel
　　　　uplifts
　　　　Such a music, so clear,
　　　　It may seem in God's ear
Worth more than a woman's hoarse weeping? And thus,
Pity tender as tears, I above thee would speak,
Thou woman that weepest! weep unscorned of us!
I, the tearless and pure, am but loving and weak.

Ador. Speak low, my brother, low,—and not of love
Or human or angelic!　Rather stand
Before the throne of that Supreme above,
In whose infinitude the secrecies
Of thine own being lie hid, and lift thine hand
Exultant, saying, ' Lord God, I am wise!'—
Than utter *here*, ' I love.'

Zerah.　　　　　　And yet thine eyes
Do utter it.　They melt in tender light,
The tears of heaven.

Ador.　　　　　　Of heaven.　Ah me!

Zerah. Ador!

Ador.   Say on !

Zerah.   The crucified are three.
Beloved, they are unlike.

Ador.   Unlike.

Zerah.   For one
        Is as a man who has sinned and still
            Doth wear the wicked will,
        The hard malign life-energy,
Tossed outward, in the parting soul's disdain,
On brow and lip that cannot change again.

Ador. And one—

Zerah.   Has also sinned.
And yet, (O marvel !) doth the Spirit-wind
Blow white those waters ?   Death upon his face
        Is rather shine than shade,
A tender shine by looks beloved made :
He seemeth dying in a quiet place,
And less by iron wounds in hands and feet
Than heart-broke by new joy too sudden and sweet.

Ador. And ONE !—

Zerah.   And ONE !—

Ador.   Why dost thou pause ?

Zerah.   God ! God !
        Spirit of my spirit ! who movest
Through seraph veins in burning deity
To light the quenchless pulses !—

Ador.   But hast trod
The depths of love in thy peculiar nature,
And not in any thou hast made and lovest

In narrow seraph hearts!—

Zerah.   Above, Creator!

Within, Upholder!

Ador.   And below, below,

The creature's and the upholden's sacrifice!

Zerah. Why do I pause?—

Ador.   There is a silentness

    That answers thee enow,

    That, like a brazen sound

Excluding others, doth ensheathe us round,—

Hear it.   It is not from the visible skies

    Though they are still,

Unconscious that their own dropped dews express

The light of heaven on every earthly hill.

It is not from the hills, though calm and bare

    They, since their first creation,

Through midnight cloud or morning's glittering air

Or the deep deluge blindness, toward the place

Whence thrilled the mystic word's creative grace,

    And whence again shall come

    The word that uncreates,

Have lift their brows in voiceless expectation.

It is not from the places that entomb

Man's dead, though common Silence there dilates

Her soul to grand proportions, worthily

    To fill life's vacant room.

    Not there: not there.

Not yet within those chambers lieth He,

A dead one in his living world; his south

And west winds blowing over earth and sea,
And not a breath on that creating mouth.
       But now,—a silence keeps
       (Not death's, nor sleep's)
       The lips whose whispered word
Might roll the thunders round reverberated.
       Silent art thou, O my Lord,
       Bowing down thy stricken head!
       Fearest thou, a groan of thine
Would make the pulse of thy creation fail
As thine own pulse?—would rend the veil
Of visible things and let the flood
Of the unseen Light, the essential God,
Rush in to whelm the undivine?
Thy silence, to my thinking, is as dread.
  Zerah. O silence!
  Ador.   Doth it say to thee—the NAME,
Slow-learning seraph?
  Zerah   I have learnt.
  Ador.   The flame
Perishes in thine eyes.
  Zerah.   He opened his,
And looked. I cannot bear—
  Ador.   Their agony?
  Zerah. Their love. God's depth is in them. From
    his brows
White, terrible in meekness, didst thou see
       The lifted eyes unclose?
He is God, seraph! Look no more on me,
O God—I am not God.

Ador.   The loving is
Sublimed within them by the sorrowful.
In heaven we could sustain them.
    Zerah.   Heaven is dull,
Mine Ador, to man's earth.   The light that burns
       In fluent, refluent motion
       Along the crystal ocean ;
The springing of the golden harps between
The bowery wings, in fountains of sweet sound
The winding, wandering music that returns
Upon itself, exultingly self-bound
In the great spheric round
       Of everlasting praises ;
The God-thoughts in our midst that intervene,
Visibly flashing from the súpreme throne
       Full in seraphic faces
Till each astonishes the other, grown
More beautiful with worship and delight—
My heaven ! my home of heaven ! my infinite
Heaven-choirs ! what are ye to this dust and death,
This cloud, this cold, these tears, this failing breath.
Where God's immortal love now issueth
       In this MAN's woe ?
    Ador. His eyes are very deep yet calm.
    Zerah.   No more
On *me*, Jehovah-man—
    Ador.   Calm-deep.   They show
A passion which is tranquil.   They are seeing
No earth, no heaven, no men that slay and curse,

No seraphs that adore;
Their gaze is on the invisible, the dread,
The things we cannot view or think or speak,
Because we are too happy, or too weak,—
The sea of ill, for which the universe
With all its pilëd space, can find no shore,
With all its life, no living foot to tread.
But he, accomplished in Jehovah-being,
     Sustains the gaze adown,
     Conceives the vast despair,
And feels the billowy griefs come up to drown.
Nor fears, nor faints, nor fails, till all be finished.

   Zerah. Thus, do I find Thee thus? My undiminished
And undiminishable God!—my God!
The echoes are still tremulous along
The heavenly mountains, of the latest song
Thy manifested glory swept abroad
In rushing past our lips: they echo aye
     ' Creator, thou art strong!
Creator, thou art blessed over all.'
By what new utterance shall I now recall,
Unteaching the heaven-echoes? dare I say,
' Creator, thou art feebler than thy work!
Creator, thou art sadder than thy creature!
     A worm, and not a man,
     Yea, no worm, but a curse?'
I dare not so mine heavenly phrase reverse.
Albeit the piercing thorn and thistle-fork
     (Whose seed disordered ran

From Eve's hand trembling when the curse did reach her)
Be garnered darklier in thy soul, the rod
That smites thee never blossoming, and thou
Grief-bearer for thy world, with unkinged brow—
I leave to men their song of Ichabod :
I have an angel-tongue—I know but praise.

   Ador. Hereafter shall the blood-bought captives raise
The passion-song of blood.

   Zerah.   And *we*, extend
Our holy vacant hands towards the Throne,
Crying ' We have no music.'

   Ador.   Rather, blend
     Both musics into one.
The sanctities and sanctified above
Shall each to each, with lifted looks serene,
     Their shining faces lean,
     And mix the adoring breath
And breathe the full thanksgiving.

   Zerah.   But the love—
The love, mine Ador !

   Ador.   Do we love not ?

   Zerah.   Yea,
But not as man shall ! not with life for death,
New-throbbing through the startled being ; not
With strange astonished smiles, that ever may
Gush passionate like tears and fill their place :
Nor yet with speechless memories of what
Earth's winters were, enverduring the green
     Of every heavenly palm

Whose windless, shadeless calm
Moves only at the breath of the Unseen.
Oh, not with this blood on us—and this face,—
Still, haply, pale with sorrow that it bore
In our behalf, and tender evermore
With nature all our own, upon us gazing—
Nor yet with these forgiving hands upraising
Their unreproachful wounds, alone to bless!
Alas, Creator! shall we love Thee less
Than mortals shall?

   Ador.   Amen! so let it be.
We love in our proportion, to the bound
Thine infinite our finite set around,
And that is finitely,— thou, infinite
And worthy infinite love!   And our delight
Is, watching the dear love poured out to thee
From ever fuller chalice.   Blessed they,
Who love thee more than we do: blessed we,
Viewing that love which shall exceed even this,
And winning in the sight a double bliss
For all so lost in love's supremacy.
The bliss is better.   Only on the sad
    Cold earth there are who say
It seemeth better to be great than glad.
The bliss is better.   Love him more, O man,
    Than sinless seraphs can!

  Zerah. Yea, love him more!
  Voices of the angelic multitude. Yea, more!
  Ador.   The loving word

Is caught by those from whom we stand apart.
For silence hath no deepness in her heart
Where love's low name low breathed would not be heard
By angels, clear as thunder.

   Angelic voices.   Love him more!

   Ador. Sweet voices, swooning o'er
       The music which ye make!
   Albeit to love there were not ever given
   A mournful sound when uttered out of heaven,
   That angel-sadness ye would fitly take.
   Of love be silent now! we gaze adown
   Upon the incarnate Love who wears no crown.

Zerah. No crown! the woe instead
      Is heavy on his head,
      Pressing inward on his brain
      With a hot and clinging pain
      Till all tears are prest away,
   And clear and calm his vision may
      Peruse the black abyss.
      No rod, no sceptre is
   Holden in his fingers pale;
   They close instead upon the nail,
      Concealing the sharp dole,
   Never stirring to put by
      The fair hair peaked with blood,
   Drooping forward from the rood
      Helplessly, heavily
   On the cheek that waxeth colder,
   Whiter ever, and the shoulder

Where the government was laid.
His glory made the heavens afraid;
Will he not unearth this cross from its hole?
His pity makes his piteous state;
Will he be uncompassionate
  Alone to his proper soul?
  Yea, will he not lift up
  His lips from the bitter cup,
  His brows from the dreary weight,
  His hand from the clenching cross,
Crying, 'My Father, give to me
Again the joy I had with thee
Or ere this earth was made for loss?
    No stir: no sound.
The love and woe being interwound
  He cleaveth to the woe;
And putteth forth heaven's strength below,
    To bear.

Ador. And that creates his anguish now,
Which made his glory there.

  Zerah. Shall it need be so?
  Awake, thou Earth! behold.
  Thou, uttered forth of old
  In all thy life-emotion,
  In all thy vernal noises,
  In the rollings of thine ocean.
  Leaping founts, and rivers running,—
  In thy woods' prophetic heaving
  Ere the rains a stroke have given,

In thy winds' exultant voices
When they feel the hills anear,
In the firmamental sunning,
And the tempest which rejoices
Thy full heart with an awful cheer.
Thou, uttered forth of old
And with all thy music rolled
In a breath abroad
By the breathing God,—
Awake! He is here! behold!
Even *thou*—
        bescems it good
To thy vacant vision dim,
That the deadly ruin should,
For thy sake, encompass him?
That the Master-word should lie
A mere silence, while his own
        Processive harmony,
The faintest echo of his lightest tone,
Is sweeping in a choral triumph by?
        Awake! emit a cry!
        And say, albeit used
        From Adam's ancient years
        To falls of acrid tears,
        To frequent sighs unloosed,
        Caught back to press again
        On bosoms zoned with pain—
        To corses still and sullen
        The shine and music dulling

With closèd eyes and ears
That nothing sweet can enter,
Commoving thee no less
With that forced quietness
Than the earthquake in thy centre—
Thou hast not learnt to bear
This new divine despair!
These tears that sink into thee,
These dying eyes that view thee,
This dropping blood from lifted rood,
They darken and undo thee.
Thou canst not presently sustain this corse—
Cry, cry, thou hast not force!
Cry, thou wouldst fainer keep
Thy hopeless charnels deep,
Thyself a general tomb
Where the first and the second Death
Sit gazing face to face
And mar each other's breath,
While silent bones through all the place
'Neath sun and moon do faintly glisten
And seem to lie and listen
For the tramp of the coming Doom.
Is it not meet
That they who erst the Eden fruit did eat,
Should champ the ashes?
That they who wrap them in the thunder-cloud
Should wear it as a shroud,
Perishing by its flashes?

That they who vexed the lion, should be rent?
Cry, cry 'I will sustain my punishment,
The sin being mine; but take away from me
This visioned Dread—this Man—this Deity!'
The Earth. I have groaned; I have travailed: I am
        weary.
I am blind with my own grief, and cannot see,
As clear-eyed angels can, his agony,
And what I see I also can sustain,
Because his power protects me from his pain.
I have groaned; I have travailed: I am dreary,
Harkening the thick sobs of my children's heart:
        How can I say 'Depart'
To that Atoner making calm and free?
        Am I a God as he,
To lay down peace and power as willingly?
Ador. He looked for some to pity.   There is none
All pity is within him and not for him.
His earth is iron under him, and o'er him
        His skies are brass.
        His seraphs cry 'Alas'
With hallelujah voice that cannot weep.
And man, for whom the dreadful work is done . . .
Scornful voices from the Earth. If verily this *be* the
        Eternal's son—
Ador. Thou hearest.   Man is grateful.
Zerah.   Can I hear
Nor darken into man and cease for ever
        My seraph-smile to wear?

Was it for such,
It pleased him to overleap
His glory with his love and sever
From the God-light and the throne
And all angels bowing down,
For whom his every look did touch
New notes of joy on the unworn string
Of an eternal worshipping ?
For such, he left his heaven ?
There, though never bought by blood
And tears, we gave him gratitude :
We loved him there, though unforgiven.

Ador.   The light is riven
Above, around,
And down in lurid fragments flung,
That catch the mountain-peak and stream
With momentary gleam,
Then perish in the water and the ground.
River and waterfall,
Forest and wilderness,
Mountain and city, are together wrung
Into one shape, and that is shapelessness ;
The darkness stands for all.

Zerah. The pathos hath the day undone :
The death-look of His eyes
Hath overcome the sun
And made it sicken in its narrow skies.

Ador. Is it to death ?   He dieth.

Zerah.   Through the dark

He still, he only, is discernible—
The naked hands and feet transfixéd stark,
The countenance of patient anguish white,
    Do make themselves a light
More dreadful than the glooms which round them dwell,
And therein do they shine.

   Ador.   God! Father-God!
Perpetual Radiance on the radiant throne!
Uplift the lids of inward deity,
    Flashing abroad
     Thy burning Infinite.
Light up this dark where there is nought to see
Except the unimagined agony
Upon the sinless forehead of the Son!

   Zerah. God, tarry not! Behold, enow
Hath he wandered as a stranger,
Sorrowed as a victim. Thou
    Appear for him O Father!
    Appear for him, Avenger!
Appear for him, just One and holy One,
    For he is holy and just!
At once the darkness and dishonour rather
To the ragged jaws of hungry chaos rake,
  And hurl aback to ancient dust
  These mortals that make blasphemies
  With their made breath, this earth and skies
    That only grow a little dim,
    Seeing their curse on him.
    But him, of all forsaken,

Of creature and of brother,
Never wilt thou forsake!
Thy living and thy loving cannot slacken
Their firm essential hold upon each other,
And well thou dost remember how his part
Was still to lie upon thy breast and be
Partaker of the light that dwelt in thee
Ere sun or seraph shone;
And how while silence trembled round the throne
Thou countedst by the beatings of his heart
The moments of thine own eternity.
Awaken,
O right hand with the lightnings! Again gather
His glory to thy glory! What estranger,
What ill supreme in evil, can be thrust
Between the faithful Father and the Son?
Appear for him, O Father!
Appear for him, Avenger!
Appear for him, just one and holy one,
For he is holy and just!

Ador. Thy face upturned toward the throne is
dark;
Thou hast no answer, Zerah.

Zerah. No reply,
O unforsaking Father?

Ador. Hark!
Instead of downward voice, a cry
Is uttered from beneath.

Zerah. And by a sharper sound than death,

Mine immortality is riven.
The heavy darkness which doth tent the sky
Floats backward as by a sudden wind ·
   But I see no light behind,
    But I feel the farthest stars are all
     Stricken and shaken,
And I know a shadow sad and broad
     Doth fall—doth fall
On our vacant thrones in heaven.
    Voice from the Cross. MY GOD, MY GOD,
WHY HAST THOU ME FORSAKEN?
    The Earth. Ah me, ah me, ah me! the dreadful
     why!
My sin is on thee, sinless one!   Thou art
God-orphaned, for my burden on thy head.
Dark sin, white innocence, endurance dread!
Be still, within your shrouds, my buried dead ;
Nor work with this quick horror round mine heart.
    Zerah. *He* hath forsaken *him.*   I perish.
    Ador.   Hold
Upon his name! we perish not.   Of old
His will—
    Zerah. I seek his will.   Seek, seraphim!
My God, my God! where is it?   Doth that curse
Reverberate spare us, seraph or universe?
     He hath forsaken *him.*
    Ador. He cannot fail.
    Angel Voices. We faint, we droop,
      Our love doth tremble like fear

Voices of Fallen Angels from the earth. Do we pre-
    vail?
Or are we lost?   Hath not the ill we did
    Been heretofore our good?
Is it not ill that one, all sinless, should
Hang heavy with all curses on a cross?
Nathless, that cry!   With huddled faces hid
Within the empty graves which men did scoop
To hold more damnëd dead, we shudder through
    What shall exalt us or undo,
    Our triumph, or our loss.
Voice from the Cross. IT IS FINISHED.
Zerah.   Hark, again!
    Like a victor, speaks the slain.
Angel Voices. Finished be the trembling vain!
Ador. Upward, like a well-loved son,
    Looketh He, the orphaned one.
Angel Voices. Finished is the mystic pain.
Voices of Fallen Angels. His deathly forehead at the
      word,
    Gleameth like a seraph sword.
Angel Voices. Finished is the demon reign.
Ador. His breath, as living God, createth,
    His breath, as dying man, completeth.
Angel Voices. Finished work his hands sustain.
The Earth. In mine ancient sepulchres
    Where my kings and prophets freeze,
    Adam dead four thousand years,
    Unwakened by the universe's

Everlasting moan,
Aye his ghastly silence mocking—
Unwakened by his children's knocking
At his old sepulchral stone,
   'Adam, Adam, all this curse is
   Thine and on us yet!'—
Unwakened by the ceaseless tears
Wherewith they made his cerement wet,
   'Adam, must thy curse remain?'—
Starts with sudden life and hears
Through the slow dripping of the caverned caves,—
Angel Voices. Finished is his bane.
   Voice from the Cross. FATHER! MY SPIRIT TO THINE
      HANDS IS GIVEN.
Ador. Hear the wailing winds that be
By wings of unclean spirits made!
   They, in that last look, surveyed
The love they lost in losing heaven,
      And passionately flee
   With a desolate cry that cleaves
   The natural storms—though *they* are lifting
God's strong cedar-roots like leaves,
   And the earthquake and the thunder,
   Neither keeping either under,
   Roar and hurtle through the glooms—
   And a few pale stars are drifting
   Past the dark, to disappear,
   What time, from the splitting tombs
   Gleamingly the dead arise,

Viewing with their death-calmed eyes
The elemental strategies,
To witness, victory is the Lord's.
Hear the wail o' the spirits! hear!
   Zerah. I hear alone the memory of his words.

EPILOGUE.

I.

My song is done.
My voice that long hath faltered shall be still.
The mystic darkness drops from Calvary's hill
Into the common light of this day's sun.

II.

I see no more thy cross, O holy Slain!
I hear no more the horror and the coil
   Of the great world's turmoil
Feeling thy countenance *too still*,—nor yell
Of demons sweeping past it to their prison.
The skies that turned to darkness with thy pain
   Make now a summer's day;
And on my changèd ear that sabbath bell
   Records how CHRIST IS RISEN.

III.

And I—ah! what am I
To counterfeit, with faculty earth-darkened,

Seraphic brows of light
And seraph language never used nor harkened?
Ah me! what word that seraphs say, could come
From mouth so used to sighs, so soon to lie
Sighless, because then breathless, in the tomb?

IV.

Bright ministers of God and grace—of grace
Because of God! whether ye bow adown
In your own heaven, before the living face
Of him who died and deathless wears the crown,
Or whether at this hour ye haply are
Anear, around me, hiding in the night
Of this permitted ignorance your light,
   This feebleness to spare,—
Forgive me, that mine earthly heart should dare
Shape images of unincarnate spirits
And lay upon their burning lips a thought
Cold with the weeping which mine earth inherits.
And though ye find in such hoarse music, wrought
To copy yours, a cadence all the while
Of sin and sorrow—only pitying smile!
   Ye know to pity, well.

V.

I too may haply smile another day
At the far recollection of this lay,

When God may call me in your midst to dwell,
To hear your most sweet music's miracle
And see your wondrous faces.   May it be!
For his remembered sake, the Slain on rood,
Who rolled his earthly garment red in blood
(Treading the wine-press) that the weak, like me,
Before his heavenly throne should walk in white.

PROMETHEUS BOUND.

FROM THE GREEK OF ÆSCHYLUS.

PROMETHEUS BOUND.

— ♦ —

PERSONS OF THE DRAMA.

PROMETHEUS.   HEPHÆSTUS.
OCEANUS.   Io, daughter of Inachus.
HERMES.   STRENGTH and FORCE.
CHORUS of Ocean Nymphs.

SCENE.—STRENGTH and FORCE, HEPHÆSTUS and PROMETHEUS,
at the Rocks.

Strength. We reach the utmost limit of the earth,
The Scythian track, the desert without man.
And now, Hephæstus, thou must needs fulfil
The mandate of our Father, and with links
Indissoluble of adamantine chains
Fasten against this beetling precipice
This guilty god.   Because he filched away
Thine own bright flower, the glory of plastic fire,
And gifted mortals with it,—such a sin
It doth behove he expiate to the gods,
Learning to accept the empery of Zeus
And leave off his old trick of loving man.

   Hephæstus. O Strength and Force, for you, our
       Zeus's will
Presents a deed for doing, no more!—but I,

I lack your daring, up this storm-rent chasm
To fix with violent hands a kindred god,
Howbeit necessity compels me so
That I must dare it, and our Zeus commands
With a most inevitable word. Ho, thou!
High-thoughted son of Themis who is sage!
Thee loth, I loth must rivet fast in chains
Against this rocky height unclomb by man,
Where never human voice nor face shall find
Out thee who lov'st them, and thy beauty's flower,
Scorched in the sun's clear heat, shall fade away.
Night shall come up with garniture of stars
To comfort thee with shadow, and the sun
Disperse with retrickt beams the morning-frosts,
But through all changes sense of present woe
Shall vex thee sore, because with none of them
There comes a hand to free.   Such fruit is plucked
From love of man! and in that thou, a god,
Didst brave the wrath of gods and give away
Undue respect to mortals, for that crime
Thou art adjudged to guard this joyless rock,
Erect, unslumbering, bending not the knee,
And many a cry and unavailing moan
To utter on the air.   For Zeus is stern
And new-made kings are cruel.
   Strength.   Be it so.
Why loiter in vain pity?   Why not hate
A god the gods hate? one too who betrayed
Thy glory unto men?

Hephæstus.   An awful thing
Is kinship joined to friendship.
   Strength.   Grant it be;
Is disobedience to the Father's word
A possible thing?   Dost quail not more for that?
   Hephæstus. Thou, at least, art a stern one: ever bold.
   Strength. Why, if I wept, it were no remedy;
And do not *thou* spend labour on the air
To bootless uses.
   Hephæstus.   Cursed handicraft!
I curse and hate thee, O my craft!
   Strength.   Why hate
Thy craft most plainly innocent of all
These pending ills?
   Hephæstus.   I would some other hand
Were here to work it!
   Strength.   All work hath its pain,
Except to rule the gods.   There is none free
Except King Zeus.
   Hephæstus.   I know it very well:
I argue not against it.
   Strength.   Why not, then,
Make haste and lock the fetters over HIM
Lest Zeus behold thee lagging?
   Hephæstus.   Here be chains.
Zeus may behold these.
   Strength.   Seize him: strike amain:
Strike with the hammer on each side his hands—
Rivet him to the rock.

Hephæstus.   The work is done,
And thoroughly done.
　Strength.   Still faster grapple him ;
Wedge him in deeper : leave no inch to stir.
He's terrible for finding a way out
From the irremediable.
　Hephæstus   Here's an arm, at least,
Grappled past freeing.
　Strength.   Now then, buckle me
The other securely.   Let this wise one learn
He's duller than our Zeus.
　Hephæsius.   Oh, none but he
Accuse me justly.
　Strength.   Now, straight through the chest,
Take him and bite him with the clenching tooth
Of the adamantine wedge, and rivet him.
　Hephæstus. Alas, Prometheus, what thou sufferest
　　here
I sorrow over.
　Strength.   Dost thou flinch again
And breathe groans for the enemies of Zeus ?
Beware lest thine own pity find thee out.
　Hephæstus. Thou dost behold a spectacle that turns
The sight o' the eyes to pity.
　Strength.   I behold
A sinner suffer his sin's penalty.
But lash the thongs about his sides.
　Hephæstus.   So much,
I must do.   Urge no farther than I must.

Strength. Ay, but I *will* urge!—and, with shout on
    shout,
Will hound thee at this quarry.   Get thee down
And ring amain the iron round his legs.

   Hephæstus. That work was not long doing.

   Strength.   Heavily now
Let fall the strokes upon the perforant gyves:
For He who rates the work has a heavy hand.

   Hephæstus. Thy speech is savage as thy shape.

   Strength.   Be thou
Gentle and tender! but revile not me
For the firm will and the untruckling hate.

   Hephæstus. Let us go.   He is netted round with
    chains.

   Strength. Here, now, taunt on! and having spoiled
    the gods
Of honours, crown withal thy mortal men
Who live a whole day out.   Why how could *they*
Draw off from thee one single of thy griefs?
Methinks the Dæmons gave thee a wrong name,
Prometheus, which means Providence,—because
Thou dost thyself need providence to see
Thy roll and ruin from the top of doom.

   Prometheus (alone). O holy Æther, and swift-wingèd
    Winds,
And River-wells, and laughter innumerous
Of yon sea-waves!   Earth, mother of us all,
And all-viewing cyclic Sun, I cry on you,—
Behold me a god, what I endure from gods!

Behold, with throe on throe
How, wasted by this woe,
I wrestle down the myriad years of time !
Behold, how fast around me,
The new King of the happy ones sublime
Has flung the chain he forged, has shamed and
    bound me !
Woe, woe ! to-day's woe and the coming morrow's
I cover with one groan.   And where is found me
    A limit to these sorrows ?
And yet what word do I say ?   I have foreknown
Clearly all things that should be ; nothing done
Comes sudden to my soul ; and I must bear
What is ordained with patience, being aware
Necessity doth front the universe
With an invincible gesture.   Yet this curse
Which strikes me now, I find it hard to brave
In silence or in speech.   Because I gave
Honour to mortals, I have yoked my soul
To this compelling fate.   Because I stole
The secret fount of fire, whose bubbles went
Over the ferule's brim, and manward sent
Art's mighty means and perfect rudiment,
That sin I expiate in this agony,
Hung here in fetters, 'neath the blanching sky.
    Ah, ah me ! what a sound,
What a fragrance sweeps up from a pinion unseen
Of a god, or a mortal, or nature between,
Sweeping up to this rock where the earth has her bound,

To have sight of my pangs or some guerdon obtain.
Lo, a god in the anguish, a god in the chain!
    The god, Zeus hateth sore
    And his gods hate again,
As many as tread on his glorified floor,
Because I loved mortals too much evermore.
Alas me! what a murmur and motion I hear,
    As of birds flying near!
    And the air undersings
    The light stroke of their wings—
And all life that approaches I wait for in fear.

Chorus of sea nymphs, 1st strophe.

    Fear nothing! our troop
    Floats lovingly up
    With a quick-oaring stroke
    Of wings steered to the rock,
Having softened the soul of our father below.
For the gales of swift-bearing have sent me a sound,
And the clank of the iron, the malleted blow,
    Smote down the profound
    Of my caverns of old,
And struck the red light in a blush from my brow,—
Till I sprang up unsandaled, in haste to behold,
And rushed forth on my chariot of wings manifold.

Prometheus. Alas me!—alas me!
Ye offspring of Tethys who bore at her breast
Many children, and eke of Oceanus, he

Coiling still around earth with perpetual unrest!
   Behold me and see
  How transfixed with the fang
  Of a fetter I hang
On the high-jutting rocks of this fissure and keep
An uncoveted watch o'er the world and the deep.

Chorus, 1st antistrophe.

I behold thee, Prometheus; yet now, yet now,
A terrible cloud whose rain is tears
Sweeps over mine eyes that witness how
   Thy body appears
Hung awaste on the rocks by infrangible chains:
For new is the Hand, new the rudder that steers
The ship of Olympus through surge and wind—
And of old things passed, no track is behind.

Prometheus. Under earth, under Hades
  Where the home of the shade is,
 All into the deep, deep Tartarus,
  I would he had hurled me adown.
I would he had plunged me, fastened thus
In the knotted chain with the savage clang,
All into the dark where there should be none,
Neither god nor another, to laugh and see.
  But now the winds sing through and shake
  The hurtling chains wherein I hang,
  And I, in my naked sorrows, make
   Much mirth for my enemy.

Chorus, 2nd strophe.

Nay! who of the gods hath a heart so stern
  As to use thy woe for a mock and mirth?
Who would not turn more mild to learn
  Thy sorrows? who of the heaven and earth
      Save Zeus? But he
      Right wrathfully
Bears on his sceptral soul unbent
And rules thereby the heavenly seed,
Nor will he pause till he content
His thirsty heart in a finished deed;
Or till Another shall appear,
To win by fraud, to seize by fear
The hard-to-be-captured government.

Prometheus. Yet even of *me* he shall have need,
  That monarch of the blessed seed,
  Of me, of me, who now am cursed
    By his fetters dire,—
  To wring my secret out withal
    And learn by whom his sceptre shall
Be filched from him—as was, at first,
      His heavenly fire.
  But he never shall enchant me
    With his honey-lipped persuasion;
  Never, never shall he daunt me
    With the oath and threat of passion
  Into speaking as they want me,
  Till he loose this savage chain,

And accept the expiation
Of my sorrow, in his pain.

Chorus, 2nd antistrophe.

Thou art, sooth, a brave god,
    And, for all thou hast borne
From the stroke of the rod,
    Nought relaxest from scorn.
But thou speakest unto me
    Too free and unworn;
And a terror strikes through me
    And festers my soul
    And I fear, in the roll
Of the storm, for thy fate
    In the ship far from shore:
Since the son of Saturnus is hard in his hate
    And unmoved in his heart evermore.

Prometheus. I know that Zeus is stern;
I know he metes his justice by his will;
And yet, his soul shall learn
More softness when once broken by this ill:
And curbing his unconquerable vaunt
He shall rush on in fear to meet with me
Who rush to meet with him in agony,
To issues of harmonious covenant.

Chorus. Remove the veil from all things and relate
The story to us,—of what crime accused,
Zeus smites thee with dishonourable pangs.

Speak : if to teach us do not grieve thyself.

 Prometheus. The utterance of these things is torture
   to me,
But so, too, is their silence; each way lies
Woe strong as fate.

     When gods began with wrath,
And war rose up between their starry brows,
Some choosing to cast Chronos from his throne
That Zeus might king it there, and some in haste
With opposite oaths that they would have no Zeus
To rule the gods for ever,—I, who brought
The counsel I thought meetest, could not move
The Titans, children of the Heaven and Earth,
What time, disdaining in their rugged souls
My subtle machinations, they assumed
It was an easy thing for force to take
The mastery of fate. My mother, then,
Who is called not only Themis but Earth too,
(Her single beauty joys in many names)
Did teach me with reiterant prophecy
What future should be, and how conquering gods
Should not prevail by strength and violence
But by guile only. When I told them so,
They would not deign to contemplate the truth
On all sides round; whereat I deemed it best
To lead my willing mother upwardly
And set my Themis face to face with Zeus
As willing to receive her. Tartarus,
With its abysmal cloister of the Dark,

Because I gave that counsel, covers up
The antique Chronos and his siding hosts,
And, by that counsel helped, the king of gods
Hath recompensed me with these bitter pangs:
For kingship wears a cancer at the heart,—
Distrust in friendship.   Do ye also ask
What crime it is for which he tortures me?
That shall be clear before you.   When at first
He filled his father's throne, he instantly
Made various gifts of glory to the gods
And dealt the empire out.   Alone of men,
Of miserable men, he took no count,
But yearned to sweep their track off from the world
And plant a newer race there.   Not a god
Resisted such desire except myself.
I dared it!   *I* drew mortals back to light,
From meditated ruin deep as hell!
For which wrong, I am bent down in these pangs
Dreadful to suffer, mournful to behold,
And I, who pitied man, am thought myself
Unworthy of pity; while I render out
Deep rhythms of anguish 'neath the harping hand
That strikes me thus—a sight to shame your Zeus!
   Chorus. Hard as thy chains and cold as all these
       rocks
Is he, Prometheus, who withholds his heart
From joining in thy woe.   I yearned before
To fly this sight; and, now I gaze on it
I sicken inwards.

Prometheus.   To my friends, indeed,
I must be a sad sight.

Chorus.   And didst thou sin
No more than so?

Prometheus.   I did restrain besides
My mortals from premeditating death.

    Chorus. How didst thou medicine the plague-fear of
      death?

    Prometheus. I set blind Hopes to inhabit in their
      house.

    Chorus. By that gift thou didst help thy mortals
      well.

    Prometheus. I gave them also fire.

    Chorus.   And have they now,
Those creatures of a day, the red-eyed fire?

    Prometheus. They have: and shall learn by it many
      arts.

    Chorus. And truly for such sins Zeus tortures thee
And will remit no anguish? Is there set
No limit before thee to thine agony?

    Prometheus. No other: only what seems good to HIM.

    Chorus. And how will it seem good? what hope re-
      mains?
Seest thou not that thou hast sinned? But that thou
      hast sinned
It glads me not to speak of, and grieves thee:
Then let it pass from both, and seek thyself
Some outlet from distress.

    Prometheus.   It is in truth

An easy thing to stand aloof from pain
And lavish exhortation and advice
On one vexed sorely by it. I have known
All in prevision. By my choice, my choice,
I freely sinned—I will confess my sin—
And helping mortals, found mine own despair.
I did not think indeed that I should pine
Beneath such pangs against such skiey rocks,
Doomed to this drear hill and no neighbouring
Of any life : but mourn not ye for griefs
I bear to-day : hear rather, dropping down
To the plain, how other woes creep on to me,
And learn the consummation of my doom.
Beseech you, nymphs, beseech you, grieve for me
Who now am grieving; for Grief walks the earth,
And sits down at the foot of each by turns.

   Chorus. We hear the deep clash of thy words,
       Prometheus, and obey.
  And I spring with a rapid foot away
  From the rushing car and the holy air,
      The track of birds ;
  And I drop to the rugged ground and there
    Await the tale of thy despair.

        OCEANUS *enters.*

  Oceanus. I reach the bourn of my weary road
    Where I may see and answer thee,
    Prometheus, in thine agony.
  On the back of the quick-winged bird I glode,

And I bridled him in
With the will of a god.
Behold, thy sorrow aches in me
Constrained by the force of kin.
Nay, though that tie were all undone,
For the life of none beneath the sun
Would I seek a larger benison
Than I seek for thine.
And thou shalt learn my words are truth,—
That no fair parlance of the mouth
Grows falsely out of mine.
Now give me a deed to prove my faith ;
For no faster friend is named in breath
Than I, Oceanus, am thine.
Prometheus. Ha ! what has brought thee ? Hast
thou also come
To look upon my woe ? How hast thou dared
To leave the depths called after thee, the caves
Self-hewn and self-roofed with spontaneous rock,
To visit earth, the mother of my chain ?
Hast come indeed to view my doom and mourn
That I should sorrow thus ? Gaze on, and see
How I, the fast friend of your Zeus,—how I
The erector of the empire in his hand,
Am bent beneath that hand, in this despair.
Oceanus. Prometheus, I behold : and I would fain
Exhort thee, though already subtle enough,
To a better wisdom. Titan, know thyself,
And take new softness to thy manners since

A new king rules the gods. If words like these,
Harsh words and trenchant, thou wilt fling abroad,
Zeus haply, though he sit so far and high,
May hear thee do it, and so, this wrath of his
Which now affects thee fiercely, shall appear
A mere child's sport at vengeance. Wretched god,
Rather dismiss the passion which thou hast,
And seek a change from grief. Perhaps I seem
To address thee with old saws and outworn sense,—
Yet such a curse, Prometheus, surely waits
On lips that speak too proudly: thou, meantime,
Art none the meeker, nor dost yield a jot
To evil circumstance, preparing still
To swell the account of grief with other griefs
Than what are borne. Beseech thee, use me then
For counsel: do not spurn against the pricks,—
Seeing that who reigns, reigns by cruelty
Instead of right. And now, I go from hence,
And will endeavour if a power of mine
Can break thy fetters through. For thee,—be calm,
And smooth thy words from passion. Knowest thou not
Of perfect knowledge, thou who knowest too much,
That where the tongue wags, ruin never lags?

  Prometheus. I gratulate thee who hast shared and
    dared
All things with me, except their penalty.
Enough so! leave these thoughts. It cannot be
That thou shouldst move HIM. HE may *not* be moved;
And *thou*, beware of sorrow on this road.

Oceanus. Ay! ever wiser for another's use
Than thine! the event, and not the prophecy,
Attests it to me.   Yet where now I rush,
Thy wisdom hath no power to drag me back;
Because I glory, glory, to go hence
And win for thee deliverance from thy pangs,
As a free gift from Zeus.

   Prometheus.   Why there, again,
I give thee gratulation and applause.
Thou lackest no goodwill.   But, as for deeds,
Do nought! 'twere all done vainly; helping nought,
Whatever thou wouldst do.   Rather take rest
And keep thyself from evil.   If I grieve,
I do not therefore wish to multiply
The griefs of others.   Verily, not so!
For still my brother's doom doth vex my soul,—
My brother Atlas, standing in the west,
Shouldering the column of the heaven and earth,
A difficult burden!   I have also seen,
And pitied as I saw, the earth-born one,
The inhabitant of old Cilician caves,
The great war-monster of the hundred heads,
(All taken and bowed beneath the violent Hand,)
Typhon the fierce, who did resist the gods,
And, hissing slaughter from his dreadful jaws,
Flash out ferocious glory from his eyes
As if to storm the throne of Zeus.   Whereat,
The sleepless arrow of Zeus flew straight at him,
The headlong bolt of thunder breathing flame,

And struck him downward from his eminence
Of exultation; through the very soul,
It struck him, and his strength was withered up
To ashes, thunder-blasted. Now he lies
A helpless trunk supinely, at full length
Beside the strait of ocean, spurred into
By roots of Ætna; high upon whose tops
Hephæstus sits and strikes the flashing ore.
From thence the rivers of fire shall burst away
Hereafter, and devour with savage jaws
The equal plains of fruitful Sicily,
Such passion he shall boil back in hot darts
Of an insatiate fury and sough of flame,
Fallen Typhon,—howsoever struck and charred
By Zeus's bolted thunder. But for thee,
Thou art not so unlearned as to need
My teaching—let thy knowledge save thyself.
I quaff the full cup of a present doom,
And wait till Zeus hath quenched his will in wrath.

   Oceanus. Prometheus, art thou ignorant of this,
That words do medicine anger?

   Prometheus.   If the word
With seasonable softness touch the soul
And, where the parts are ulcerous, sear them not
By any rudeness.

   Oceanus.   With a noble aim
To dare as nobly—is there harm in *that?*
Dost thou discern it? Teach me.

   Prometheus.   I discern

Vain aspiration, unresultive work.

Oceanus. Then suffer me to bear the brunt of this!
Since it is profitable that one who is wise
Should seem not wise at all.

Prometheus.   And such would seem
My very crime.

Oceanus.   In truth thine argument
Sends me back home.

Prometheus.   Lest any lament for me
Should cast thee down to hate.

Oceanus.   The hate of Him
Who sits a new king on the absolute throne?

Prometheus. Beware of him, lest thine heart grieve
    by him.

Oceanus. Thy doom, Prometheus, be my teacher!

Prometheus.   Go.
Depart—beware—and keep the mind thou hast.

Oceanus. Thy words drive after, as I rush before.
Lo! my four-footed bird sweeps smooth and wide
The flats of air with balanced pinions, glad
To bend his knee at home in the ocean-stall.

                              [OCEANUS *departs*

Chorus, 1st strophe.

I moan thy fate, I moan for thee,
    Prometheus! From my eyes too tender,
Drop after drop incessantly
    The tears of my heart's pity render
My cheeks wet from their fountains free;

Because that Zeus, the stern and cold.
  Whose law is taken from his breast,
  Uplifts his sceptre manifest
  Over the gods of old.

1st antistrophe.

  All the land is moaning
With a murmured plaint to-day:
  All the mortal nations
  Having habitations
  In the holy Asia
  Are a dirge entoning
For thine honour and thy brothers',
Once majestic beyond others
  In the old belief,—
Now are groaning in the groaning
  Of thy deep-voiced grief.

2nd strophe.

Mourn the maids inhabitant
  Of the Colchian land
Who with white, calm bosoms stand
  In the battle's roar:
Mourn the Scythian tribes that haunt
The verge of earth, Mæotis' shore.

2nd antistrophe.

  Yea! Arabia's battle-crown,
  And dwellers in the beetling town

Mount Caucasus sublimely nears,—
   An iron squadron, thundering down
     With the sharp-prowed spears.

But one other before, have I seen to remain
     By invincible pain
Bound and vanquished,—one Titan! 'twas Atlas, who
     bears
In a curse from the gods, by that strength of his own
     Which he evermore wears,
The weight of the heaven on his shoulder alone,
     While he sighs up the stars;
And the tides of the ocean wail bursting their bars,—
     Murmurs still the profound,
And black Hades roars up through the chasm of the
     ground,
And the fountains of pure-running rivers moan low
     In a pathos of woe.

Prometheus. Beseech you, think not I am silent thus
Through pride or scorn. I only gnaw my heart
With meditation, seeing myself so wronged.
For see—their honours to these new-made gods,
What other gave but I, and dealt them out
With distribution? Ay—but here I am dumb!
For here, I should repeat your knowledge to you,
If I spake aught. List rather to the deeds
I did for mortals; how, being fools before,
I made them wise and true in aim of soul.
And let me tell you—not as taunting men,

But teaching you the intention of my gifts,
How, first beholding, they beheld in vain,
And hearing, heard not, but, like shapes in dreams,
Mixed all things wildly down the tedious time,
Nor knew to build a house against the sun
With wicketed sides, nor any woodcraft knew,
But lived, like silly ants, beneath the ground
In hollow caves unsunned.   There, came to them
No steadfast sign of winter, nor of spring
Flower-perfumed, nor of summer full of fruit,
But blindly and lawlessly they did all things,
Until I taught them how the stars do rise
And set in mystery, and devised for them
Number, the inducer of philosophies,
The synthesis of Letters, and, beside,
The artificer of all things, Memory,
That sweet Muse-mother.   I was first to yoke
The servile beasts in couples, carrying
An heirdom of man's burdens on their backs.
I joined to chariots, steeds, that love the bit
They champ at—the chief pomp of golden ease.
And none but I originated ships,
The seaman's chariots, wandering on the brine
With linen wings.   And I—oh, miserable!—
Who did devise for mortals all these arts,
Have no device left now to save myself
From the woe I suffer.
    Chorus.   Most unseemly woe
Thou sufferest, and dost stagger from the sense

Bewildered! like a bad leech falling sick
Thou art faint at soul, and canst not find the drugs
Required to save thyself.

Prometheus. Harken the rest,
And marvel further, what more arts and means
I did invent,—this, greatest: if a man
Fell sick, there was no cure, nor esculent
Nor chrism nor liquid, but for lack of drugs
Men pined and wasted, till I showed them all
Those mixtures of emollient remedies
Whereby they might be rescued from disease.
I fixed the various rules of mantic art,
Discerned the vision from the common dream,
Instructed them in vocal auguries
Hard to interpret, and defined as plain
The wayside omens,—flights of crook-clawed birds,—
Showed which are, by their nature, fortunate,
And which not so, and what the food of each,
And what the hates, affections, social needs,
Of all to one another,—taught what sign
Of visceral lightness, coloured to a shade,
May charm the genial gods, and what fair spots
Commend the lung and liver. Burning so
The limbs encased in fat, and the long chine,
I led my mortals on to an art abstruse,
And cleared their eyes to the image in the fire,
Erst filmed in dark. Enough said now of this.
For the other helps of man hid underground,
The iron and the brass, silver and gold,

Can any dare affirm he found them out
Before me? none, I know! unless he choose
To lie in his vaunt.   In one word learn the whole,—
That all arts came to mortals from Prometheus.

    Chorus. Give mortals now no inexpedient help,
Neglecting thine own sorrow.   I have hope still
To see thee, breaking from the fetter here,
Stand up as strong as Zeus.

    Prometheus.   This ends not thus,
The oracular fate ordains.   I must be bowed
By infinite woes and pangs, to escape this chain.
Necessity is stronger than mine art.

    Chorus. Who holds the helm of that Necessity?

    Prometheus. The threefold Fates and the unforget-
        ting Furies.

    Chorus. Is Zeus less absolute than these are?

    Prometheus.   Yea,
And therefore cannot fly what is ordained.

    Chorus. What is ordained for Zeus, except to be
A king for ever?

    Prometheus.   'Tis too early yet
For thee to learn it : ask no more.

    Chorus.   Perhaps
Thy secret may be something holy?

    Prometheus.   Turn
To another matter : this, it is not time
To speak abroad, but utterly to veil
In silence.   For by that same secret kept,
I 'scape this chain's dishonour and its woe.

Chorus, 1st strophe.

Never, oh never
May Zeus, the all-giver,
Wrestle down from his throne
In that might of his own
To antagonize mine!
Nor let me delay
As I bend on my way
Toward the gods of the shrine
Where the altar is full
Of the blood of the bull,
Near the tossing brine
Of Ocean my father.
May no sin be sped in the word that is said,
But my vow be rather
Consummated,
Nor evermore fail, nor evermore pine.

1st antistrophe.

'Tis sweet to have
Life lengthened out
With hopes proved brave
By the very doubt,
Till the spirit enfold
Those manifest joys which were foretold.
But I thrill to behold
Thee, victim doomed,
By the countless cares

And the drear despairs
　　Forever consumed,—
And all because thou, who art fearless now
　　Of Zeus above,
Didst overflow for mankind below
　　With a free-souled, reverent love.

　　Ah friend, behold and see!
What's all the beauty of humanity?
　　Can it be fair?
What's all the strength? is it strong?
　　And what hope can they bear,
These dying livers—living one day long?
　　Ah, seest thou not, my friend,
　　　How feeble and slow
　　　And like a dream, doth go
This poor blind manhood, drifted from its end?
　　And how no mortal wranglings can confuse
　　　The harmony of Zeus?

Prometheus, I have learnt these things
　From the sorrow in thy face.
　　Another song did fold its wings
　Upon my lips in other days,
　When round the bath and round the bed
　The hymeneal chant instead
　　I sang for thee, and smiled,—
　And thou didst lead, with gifts and vows,
　　Hesione, my father's child,
　To be thy wedded spouse.

Io *enters.*

Io. What land is this? what people is here?
And who is he that writhes, I see,
    In the rock-hung chain?
Now what is the crime that hath brought thee to pain?
Now what is the land—make answer free—
Which I wander through, in my wrong and fear?
    Ah! ah! ah me!
The gad-fly stingeth to agony!
O Earth, keep off that phantasm pale
Of earth-born Argus!—ah!—I quail
    When my soul descries
That herdsman with the myriad eyes
Which seem, as he comes, one crafty eye.
Graves hide him not, though he should die,
But he doggeth me in my misery
From the roots of death, on high—on high—
And along the sands of the siding deep,
All famine-worn, he follows me,
And his waxen reed doth undersound
    The waters round
And giveth a measure that giveth sleep.

    Woe, woe, woe!
Where shall my weary course be done?
What wouldst thou with me, Saturn's son?
And in what have I sinned, that I should go
Thus yoked to grief by thine hand for ever?
    Ah! ah! dost vex me so

That I madden and shiver
　　Stung through with dread?
Flash the fire down to burn me!
Heave the earth up to cover me!
Plunge me in the deep, with the salt waves over me,
　　That the sea-beasts may be fed!
O king, do not spurn me
　　　In my prayer!
For this wandering everlonger, evermore,
　　Hath overworn me,
And I know not on what shore
I may rest from my despair.

Chorus. Hearest thou what the ox-horned maiden
　　saith?
Prometheus. How could I choose but harken what
　　she saith,
The phrensied maiden?—Inachus's child?—
Who love-warms Zeus's heart, and now is lashed
By Heré's hate along the unending ways?

Io. Who taught thee to articulate that name,—
　　My father's? Speak to his child
　　By grief and shame defiled!
Who art thou, victim, thou who dost acclaim
Mine anguish in true words on the wide air,
And callest too by name the curse that came
　　From Heré unaware,
To waste and pierce me with its maddening goad?

Ah—ah—I leap
With the pang of the hungry—I bound on the road—
  I am driven by my doom—
  I am overcome
By the wrath of an enemy strong and deep!
Are any of those who have tasted pain,
  Alas! as wretched as I?
Now tell me plain, doth aught remain
For my soul to endure beneath the sky?
Is there any help to be holpen by?
If knowledge be in thee, let it be said!
  Cry aloud—cry
To the wandering, woful maid.

Prometheus. Whatever thou wouldst learn I will
  declare,—
No riddle upon my lips, but such straight words
As friends should use to each other when they talk.
Thou seest Prometheus, who gave mortals fire.
 Io. O common Help of all men, known of all,
O miserable Prometheus,—for what cause
Dost thou endure thus?
 Prometheus.   I have done with wail
For my own griefs, but lately.
 Io.   Wilt thou not
Vouchsafe the boon to me?
 Prometheus.   Say what thou wilt,
For I vouchsafe all.
 Io.   Speak then, and reveal

Who shut thee in this chasm.

Prometheus.   The will of Zeus,

The hand of his Hephæstus.

Io.   And what crime

Dost expiate so ?

Prometheus.   Enough for thee I have told

In so much only.

Io.   Nay, but show besides

The limit of my wandering, and the time

Which yet is lacking to fulfil my grief.

Prometheus. Why, not to know were better than to
     know

For such as thou.

Io.   Beseech thee, blind me not

To that which I must suffer.

Prometheus.   If I do,

The reason is not that I grudge a boon.

Io. What reason, then, prevents thy speaking out ?

Prometheus. No grudging ; but a fear to break thine
     heart.

Io. Less care for me, I pray thee.   Certainty

I count for advantage.

Prometheus.   Thou wilt have it so

And therefore I must speak.   Now hear—

Chorus.   Not yet.

Give half the guerdon my way.   Let us learn

First, what the curse is that befell the maid,—

Her own voice telling her own wasting woes :

The sequence of that anguish shall await

The teaching of thy lips.

   Prometheus.   It doth behove
That thou, Maid Io, shouldst vouchsafe to these
The grace they pray,—the more, because they are called
Thy father's sisters : since to open out
And mourn out grief where it is possible
To draw a tear from the audience, is a work
That pays its own price well.

   Io.   I cannot choose
But trust you, nymphs, and tell you all ye ask,
In clear words—though I sob amid my speech
In speaking of the storm-curse sent from Zeus,
And of my beauty, from which height it took
Its swoop on me, poor wretch! left thus deformed
And monstrous to your eyes.   For evermore
Around my virgin-chamber, wandering went
The nightly visions which entreated me
With syllabled smooth sweetness.—'Blessed maid,
Why lengthen out thy maiden hours when fate
Permits the noblest spousal in the world ?
When Zeus burns with the arrow of thy love
And fain would touch thy beauty ?—Maiden, thou
Despise not Zeus! depart to Lernè's mead
That's green around thy father's flocks and stalls,
Until the passion of the heavenly Eye
Be quenched in sight.' Such dreams did all night long
Constrain me—me, unhappy !—till I dared
To tell my father how they trod the dark
With visionary steps.   Whereat he sent

His frequent heralds to the Pythian fane,
And also to Dodona, and inquired
How best, by act or speech, to please the gods.
The same returning brought back oracles
Of doubtful sense, indefinite response,
Dark to interpret ; but at last there came
To Inachus an answer that was clear,
Thrown straight as any bolt, and spoken out—
This—' he should drive me from my home and land
And bid me wander to the extreme verge
Of all the earth—or, if he willed it not,
Should have a thunder with a fiery eye
Leap straight from Zeus to burn up all his race
To the last root of it.'   By which Loxian word
Subdued, he drove me forth and shut me out,
He loth, me loth,—but Zeus's violent bit
Compelled him to the deed : when instantly
My body and soul were changëd and distraught,
And, hornëd as ye see, and spurred along
By the fanged insect, with a maniac leap
I rushed on to Cenchrea's limpid stream
And Lernë's fountain-water.   There, the earth-born,
The herdsman Argus, most immitigable
Of wrath, did find me out, and track me out
With countless eyes set staring at my steps :
And though an unexpected sudden doom
Drew him from life, I, curse-tormented still,
Am driven from land to land before the scourge
The gods hold o'er me. ·So thou hast heard the past,

And if a bitter future thou canst tell,
Speak on. I charge thee, do not flatter me
Through pity, with false words; for, in my mind,
Deceiving works more shame than torturing doth.

Chorus.

Ah! silence here!
Nevermore, nevermore
Would I languish for
The stranger's word
To thrill in mine ear—
Nevermore for the wrong and the woe and the fear
So hard to behold,
So cruel to bear,
Piercing my soul with a double-edged sword
Of a sliding cold.
Ah Fate! ah me!
I shudder to see
This wandering maid in her agony.

Prometheus. Grief is too quick in thee and fear too
full :
Be patient till thou hast learnt the rest.
Chorus.   Speak: teach.
To those who are sad already, it seems sweet,
By clear foreknowledge to make perfect, pain.
Prometheus. The boon ye asked me first was lightly
won,—
For first ye asked the story of this maid's grief
As her own lips might tell it. Now remains

To list what other sorrows she so young
Must bear from Heré. Inachus's child,
O thou ! drop down thy soul my weighty words,
And measure out the landmarks which are set
To end thy wandering.   Toward the orient sun
First turn thy face from mine and journey on
Along the desert flats till thou shalt come
Where Scythia's shepherd peoples dwell aloft,
Perched in wheeled waggons under woven roofs,
And twang the rapid arrow past the bow—
Approach them not ; but siding in thy course
The rugged shore-rocks resonant to the sea,
Depart that country.   On the left hand dwell
The iron-workers, called the Chalybes,
Of whom beware, for certes they are uncouth
And nowise bland to strangers.   Reaching so
The stream Hybristes (well the *scorner* called),
Attempt no passage,—it is hard to pass,—
Or ere thou come to Caucasus itself,
That highest of mountains, where the river leaps
The precipice in his strength.   Thou must toil up
Those mountain-tops that neighbour with the stars,
And tread the south way, and draw near, at last,
The Amazonian host that hateth man,
Inhabitants of Themiscyra, close
Upon Thermodon, where the sea's rough jaw
Doth gnash at Salmydessa and provide
A cruel host to seamen, and to ships
A stepdame.   They with unreluctant hand

Shall lead thee on and on, till thou arrive
Just where the ocean-gates show narrowest
On the Cimmerian isthmus.   Leaving which,
Behoves thee swim with fortitude of soul
The strait Mæotis.   Ay, and evermore
That traverse shall be famous on men's lips,
That strait, called Bosphorus, the horned one's road,
So named because of thee, who so wilt pass
From Europe's plain to Asia's continent.
How think ye, nymphs ? the king of gods appears
Impartial in ferocious deeds ?   Behold!
The god desirous of this mortal's love
Hath cursed her with these wanderings. Ah, fair child,
Thou hast met a bitter groom for bridal troth!
For all thou yet hast heard, can only prove
The incompleted prelude of thy doom.

 Io. Ah, ah !

 Prometheus. Is't thy turn, now, to shriek and moan ?
How wilt thou, when thou hast harkened what remains?

 Chorus. Besides the grief thou hast told can aught
  remain ?

 Prometheus. A sea—of foredoomed evil worked to
  storm.

 Io. What boots my life, then ? why not cast myself
Down headlong from this miserable rock,
That, dashed against the flats, I may redeem
My soul from sorrow ?   Better once to die
Than day by day to suffer.

 Prometheus.   Verily,

It would be hard for thee to bear my woe
For whom it is appointed not to die.
Death frees from woe : but I before me see
In all my far prevision not a bound
To all I suffer, ere that Zeus shall fall
From being a king.

    Io.   And can it ever be
That Zeus shall fall from empire ?

    Prometheus.   *Thou*, methinks,
Wouldst take some joy to see it.

    Io.   Could I choose ?
I who endure such pangs now, by that god !

    Prometheus. Learn from me, therefore, that the
         event shall be.

    Io. By whom shall his imperial sceptred hand
Be emptied so ?

    Prometheus.   Himself shall spoil himself,
Through his idiotic counsels

    Io.   How ? declare :
Unless the word bring evil.

    Prometheus.   He shall wed ;
And in the marriage-bond be joined to grief.

    Io. A heavenly bride—or human ?   Speak it out
If it be utterable.

    Prometheus.   Why should I say which ?
It ought not to be uttered, verily.

    Io.   Then
It is his wife shall tear him from his throne ?

    Prometheus. It is his wife shall bear a son to him,

More mighty than the father.

 Io.   From this doom
Hath he no refuge?

 Prometheus.   None: or ere that I,
Loosed from these fetters—

 Io.   Yea—but who shall loose
While Zeus is adverse?

 Prometheus.   One who is born of thee:
It is ordained so.

 Io.   What is this thou sayest?
A son of mine shall liberate thee from woe?

 Prometheus. After ten generations, count three more,
And find him in the third.

 Io.   The oracle
Remains obscure.

 Prometheus.   And search it not, to learn
Thine own griefs from it.

 Io.   Point me not to a good,
To leave me straight bereaved.

 Prometheus.   I am prepared
To grant thee one of two things.

 Io.   But which two?
Set them before me; grant me power to choose.

 Prometheus. I grant it; choose now: shall I name
   aloud
What griefs remain to wound thee, or what hand
Shall save me out of mine?

 Chorus.   Vouchsafe, O god,
The one grace of the twain to her who prays;

The next to me ; and turn back neither prayer
Dishonour'd by denial.   To herself
Recount the future wandering of her feet;
Then point me to the looser of thy chain,
Because I yearn to know him.

   Prometheus.   Since ye will,
Of absolute will, this knowledge, I will set
No contrary against it, nor keep back
A word of all ye ask for.   Io, first
To thee I must relate thy wandering course
Far winding.   As I tell it, write it down
In thy soul's book of memories.   When thou hast past
The refluent bound that parts two continents,
Track on the footsteps of the orient sun
In his own fire, across the roar of seas,—
Fly till thou hast reached the Gorgonæan flats
Beside Cisthené.   There, the Phorcides,
Three ancient maidens, live, with shape of swan,
One tooth between them, and one common eye,
On whom the sun doth never look at all
With all his rays, nor evermore the moon
When she looks through the night.   Anear to whom
Are the Gorgon sisters three, enclothed with wings,
With twisted snakes for ringlets, man-abhorred:
There is no mortal gazes in their face
And gazing can breathe on.   I speak of such
To guard thee from their horror.   Ay, and list
Another tale of a dreadful sight ; beware
The Griffins, those unbarking dogs of Zeus,

Those sharp-mouthed dogs!—and the Arimaspian host
Of one-eyed horsemen, habiting beside
The river of Pluto that runs bright with gold :
Approach them not, beseech thee.   Presently
Thou'lt come to a distant land, a dusky tribe
Of dwellers at the fountain of the Sun,
Whence flows the river Æthiops ; wind along
Its banks and turn off at the cataracts,
Just as the Nile pours from the Bybline hills
His holy and sweet wave ; his course shall guide
Thine own to that triangular Nile-ground
Where, Io, is ordained for thee and thine
A lengthened exile.   Have I said in this
Aught darkly or incompletely ?—now repeat
The question, make the knowledge fuller !   Lo,
I have more leisure than I covet, here.

   Chorus. If thou canst tell us aught that's left untold,
Or loosely told, of her most dreary flight,
Declare it straight : but if thou hast uttered all,
Grant us that latter grace for which we prayed,
Remembering how we prayed it.

   Prometheus.   She has heard
The uttermost of her wandering.   There it ends.
But that she may be certain not to have heard
All vainly, I will speak what she endured
Ere coming hither, and invoke the past
To prove my prescience true.   And so—to leave
A multitude of words and pass at once
To the subject of thy course—when thou hadst gone

To those Molossian plains which sweep around
Dodona shouldering Heaven, whereby the fane
Of Zeus Thesprotian keepeth oracle,
And, wonder past belief, where oaks do wave
Articulate adjurations—(ay, the same
Saluted thee in no perplexéd phrase
But clear with glory, noble wife of Zeus
That shouldst be,—there some sweetness took thy
    sense!)
Thou didst rush further onward, stung along
The ocean-shore, toward Rhea's mighty bay
And, tost back from it, wast tost to it again
In stormy evolution :—and, know well,
In coming time that hollow of the sea
Shall bear the name Ionian and present
A monument of Io's passage through,
Unto all mortals.   Be these words the signs
Of my soul's power to look beyond the veil
Of visible things.   The rest, to you and her
I will declare in common audience, nymphs,
Returning thither where my speech brake off.
There is a town Canobus, built upon
The earth's fair margin at the mouth of Nile
And on the mound washed up by it; Io, there
Shall Zeus give back to thee thy perfect mind,
And only by the pressure and the touch
Of a hand not terrible; and thou to Zeus
Shalt bear a dusky son who shall be called
Thence, Epaphus, *Touched*.   That son shall pluck the
    fruit

Of all that land wide-watered by the flow
Of Nile; but after him, when counting out
As far as the fifth full generation, then
Full fifty maidens, a fair woman-race,
Shall back to Argos turn reluctantly,
To fly the proffered nuptials of their kin,
Their father's brothers.   These being passion-struck,
Like falcons bearing hard on flying doves,
Shall follow, hunting at a quarry of love
They should not hunt; till envious Heaven maintain
A curse betwixt that beauty and their desire,
And Greece receive them, to be overcome
In murtherous woman-war, by fierce red hands
Kept savage by the night.   For every wife
Shall slay a husband, dyeing deep in blood
The sword of a double edge— (I wish indeed
As fair a marriage-joy to all my foes!)
One bride alone shall fail to smite to death
The head upon her pillow, touched with love,
Made impotent of purpose and impelled
To choose the lesser evil,—shame on her cheeks,
Than blood-guilt on her hands: which bride shall bear
A royal race in Argos.   Tedious speech
Were needed to relate particulars
Of these things; 'tis enough that from her seed
Shall spring the strong He, famous with the bow,
Whose arm shall break my fetters off.   Behold.
My mother Themis, that old Titaness,
Delivered to me such an oracle,—

But how and when, I should be long to speak,
And thou, in hearing, wouldst not gain at all.

Io.　　Eleleu, eleleu!
　　　How the spasm and the pain
　　　And the fire on the brain
　　　　Strike, burning me through!
How the sting of the curse, all aflame as it flew,
　　　Pricks me onward again!
How my heart in its terror is spurning my breast,
And my eyes, like the wheels of a chariot, roll round!
I am whirled from my course, to the east, to the west,
In the whirlwind of phrensy all madly inwound—
And my mouth is unbridled for anguish and hate,
And my words beat in vain, in wild storms of unrest,
　　　On the sea of my desolate fate.

　　　　　　　　　　　[Io *rushes out.*

　　　　Chorus,--strophe.

Oh, wise was he, oh, wise was he
Who first within his spirit knew
And with his tongue declared it true
That love comes best that comes unto
　　　The equal of degree!
And that the poor and that the low
Should seek no love from those above,
Whose souls are fluttered with the flow
Of airs about their golden height,
Or proud because they see arow
　　　Ancestral crowns of light.

Antistrophe.

Oh, never, never may ye, Fates,
  Behold me with your awful eyes
  Lift mine too fondly up the skies
Where Zeus upon the purple waits!
  Nor let me step too near—too near
To any suitor, bright from heaven :
  Because I see, because I fear
This loveless maiden vexed and laden
By this fell curse of Heré, driven
  On wanderings dread and drear.

Epode.

Nay, grant an equal troth instead
  Of nuptial love, to bind me by !
It will not hurt, I shall not dread
  To meet it in reply.
But let not love from those above
Revert and fix me, as I said,
  With that inevitable Eye !
I have no sword to fight that fight,
I have no strength to tread that path,
I know not if my nature hath
The power to bear, I cannot see
Whither from Zeus's infinite
I have the power to flee.

Prometheus. Yet Zeus, albeit most absolute of will,
Shall turn to meekness,—such a marriage-rite

He holds in preparation, which anon
Shall thrust him headlong from his gerent seat
Adown the abysmal void, and so the curse
His father Chronos muttered in his fall,
As he fell from his ancient throne and cursed,
Shall be accomplished wholly.   No escape
From all that ruin shall the filial Zeus
Find granted to him from any of his gods,
Unless I teach him.   I the refuge know,
And I, the means.   Now, therefore, let him sit
And brave the imminent doom, and fix his faith
On his supernal noises, hurtling on
With restless hand the bolt that breathes out fire;
For these things shall not help him, none of them,
Nor hinder his perdition when he falls
To shame, and lower than patience : such a foe
He doth himself prepare against himself,
A wonder of unconquerable hate,
An organizer of sublimer fire
Than glares in lightnings, and of grander sound
Than aught the thunder rolls, outthundering it,
With power to shatter in Poseidon's fist
The trident-spear which, while it plagues the sea,
Doth shake the shores around it.   Ay, and Zeus,
Precipitated thus, shall learn at length
The difference betwixt rule and servitude.

 Chorus. Thou makest threats for Zeus of thy desires.
 Prometheus. I tell you, all these things shall be
  fulfilled

Even so as I desire them.

Chorus. Must we then
Look out for one shall come to master Zeus?

Prometheus. These chains weigh lighter than his
sorrows shall.

Chorus. How art thou not afraid to utter such words?

Prometheus. What should *I* fear, who cannot die?

Chorus. But *he*
Can visit thee with dreader woe than death's.

Prometheus. Why, let him do it! I am here, prepared
For all things and their pangs.

Chorus. The wise are they
Who reverence Adrasteia.

Prometheus. Reverence thou,
Adore thou, flatter thou, whomever reigns,
Whenever reigning! but for me, your Zeus
Is less than nothing. Let him act and reign
His brief hour out according to his will—
He will not, therefore, rule the gods too long.
But lo! I see that courier-god of Zeus,
That new-made menial of the new-crowned king:
He doubtless comes to announce to us something new.

HERMES *enters.*

Hermes. I speak to thee, the sophist, the talker
down
Of scorn by scorn, the sinner against gods,

The reverencer of men, the thief of fire,—
I speak to thee and adjure thee! Zeus requires
Thy declaration of what marriage-rite
Thus moves thy vaunt and shall hereafter cause
His fall from empire. Do not wrap thy speech
In riddles, but speak clearly! Never cast
Ambiguous paths, Prometheus, for my feet,
Since Zeus, thou may'st perceive, is scarcely won
To mercy by such means.

    Prometheus.   A speech well-mouthed
In the utterance, and full-minded in the sense,
As doth befit a servant of the gods!
New gods, ye newly reign, and think forsooth
Ye dwell in towers too high for any dart
To carry a wound there!—have I not stood by
While two kings fell from thence? and shall I not
Behold the third, the same who rules you now,
Fall, shamed to sudden ruin?—Do I seem
To tremble and quail before your modern gods?
Far be it from me!—For thyself, depart,
Re-tread thy steps in haste. To all thou hast asked
I answer nothing.

    Hermes.   Such a wind of pride
Impelled thee of yore full sail upon these rocks.

    Prometheus. I would not barter—learn thou soothly
        that!—
My suffering for thy service. I maintain
It is a nobler thing to serve these rocks
Than live a faithful slave to father Zeus.

Thus upon scorners I retort their scorn.

    Hermes. It seems that thou dost glory in thy
       despair.

    Prometheus. I glory ? would my foes did glory so,
And I stood by to see them !—naming whom,
Thou art not unremembered.

    Hermes.   Dost thou charge
Me also with the blame of thy mischance ?

    Prometheus. I tell thee I loathe the universal gods,
Who for the good I gave them rendered back
The ill of their injustice.

    Hermes.   Thou art mad—
Thou art raving, Titan, at the fever-height.

    Prometheus. If it be madness to abhor my foes,
May I be mad !

    Hermes.   If thou wert prosperous
Thou wouldst be unendurable.

    Prometheus.   Alas !

    Hermes. Zeus knows not that word.

    Prometheus.   But maturing Time
Teaches all things.

    Hermes.   Howbeit, thou hast not learnt
The wisdom yet, thou needest.

    Prometheus.   If I had,
I should not talk thus with a slave like thee.

    Hermes. No answer thou vouchsafest, I believe,
To the great Sire's requirement.

    Prometheus.   Verily
I owe him grateful service,—and should pay it.

Hermes. Why, thou dost mock me, Titan, as I stood
A child before thy face.

Prometheus.   No child, forsooth,
But yet more foolish than a foolish child,
If thou expect that I should answer aught
Thy Zeus can ask.   No torture from his hand
Nor any machination in the world
Shall force mine utterance ere he loose, himself,
These cankerous fetters from me.   For the rest,
Let him now hurl his blanching lightnings down,
And with his white-winged snows and mutterings deep
Of subterranean thunders mix all things,
Confound them in disorder.   None of this
Shall bend my sturdy will and make me speak
The name of his dethroner who shall come.

Hermes. Can this avail thee?   Look to it!

Prometheus.   Long ago
It was looked forward to, precounselled of.

Hermes. Vain god, take righteous courage! dare
     for once
To apprehend and front thine agonies
With a just prudence.

Prometheus.   Vainly dost thou chafe
My soul with exhortation, as yonder sea
Goes beating on the rock.   Oh, think no more
That I, fear-struck by Zeus to a woman's mind,
Will supplicate him, loathèd as he is,
With feminine upliftings of my hands,
To break these chains.   Far from me be the thought!

Hermes. I have indeed, methinks, said much in
    vain,
For still thy heart beneath my showers of prayers
Lies dry and hard—nay, leaps like a young horse
Who bites against the new bit in his teeth,
And tugs and struggles against the new-tried rein.—
Still fiercest in the feeblest thing of all,
Which sophism is; since absolute will disjoined
From perfect mind is worse than weak.   Behold,
Unless my words persuade thee, what a blast
And whirlwind of inevitable woe
Must sweep persuasion through thee!   For at first
The Father will split up this jut of rock
With the great thunder and the bolted flame,
And hide thy body where a hinge of stone
Shall catch it like an arm; and when thou hast
    passed
A long black time within, thou shalt come out
To front the sun while Zeus's winged hound,
The strong carnivorous eagle, shall wheel down
To meet thee, self-called to a daily feast,
And set his fierce beak in thee and tear off
The long rags of thy flesh and batten deep
Upon thy dusky liver.   Do not look
For any end moreover to this curse
Or ere some god appear, to accept thy pangs
On his own head vicarious, and descend
With unreluctant step the darks of hell
And gloomy abysses around Tartarus.

Then ponder this—this threat is not a growth
Of vain invention; it is spoken and meant;
King Zeus's mouth is impotent to lie,
Consummating the utterance by the act;
So, look to it, thou! take heed, and nevermore
Forget good counsel, to indulge self-will.

    Chorus. Our Hermes suits his reasons to the times,
At least I think so, since he bids thee drop
Self-will for prudent counsel.   Yield to him!
When the wise err, their wisdom makes their shame.

    Prometheus. Unto me the foreknower, this mandate
        of power
          He cries, to reveal it.
What's strange in my fate, if I suffer from hate
          At the hour that I feel it?
Let the locks of the lightning, all bristling and
          whitening,
          Flash, coiling me round,
While the æther goes surging 'neath thunder and
          scourging
          Of wild winds unbound!
Let the blast of the firmament whirl from its place
          The earth rooted below,
And the brine of the ocean, in rapid emotion,
          Be driven in the face
Of the stars up in heaven, as they walk to and fro!
Let him hurl me anon into Tartarus—on—
          To the blackest degree,
With Necessity's vortices strangling me down;

But he cannot join death to a fate meant for *me !*

   Hermes. Why, the words that he speaks and the
        thoughts that he thinks

    Are maniacal !—add,

If the Fate who hath bound him should loose not the
        links,

    He were utterly mad.

    Then depart ye who groan with him,

    Leaving to moan with him,—

Go in haste! lest the roar of the thunder anearing

Should blast you to idiocy, living and hearing.

   Chorus. Change thy speech for another, thy thought
        for a new,

   If to move me and teach me indeed be thy care !

For thy words swerve so far from the loyal and true

   That the thunder of Zeus seems more easy to bear.

How! couldst teach me to venture such vileness?
        behold !

   I *choose*, with this victim, this anguish foretold !

I recoil from the traitor in hate and disdain,

And I know that the curse of the treason is worse

     Than the pang of the chain.

   Hermes. Then remember, O nymphs, what I tell
        you before,

   Nor, when pierced by the arrows that Até will throw
        you,

Cast blame on your fate and declare evermore

   That Zeus thrust you on anguish he did not fore-
        show you.

Nay, verily, nay! for ye perish anon
  For your deed—by your choice.   By no blindness
      of doubt,
No abruptness of doom, but by madness alone,
  In the great net of Até, whence none cometh out,
      Ye are wound and undone.
    Prometheus. Ay! in act now, in word now no more,
      Earth is rocking in space.
And the thunders crash up with a roar upon roar,
  And the eddying lightnings flash fire in my face,
And the whirlwinds are whirling the dust round and
      round,
  And the blasts of the winds universal leap free
And blow each upon each with a passion of sound,
  And æther goes mingling in storm with the sea.
Such a curse on my head, in a manifest dread,
  From the hand of your Zeus has been hurtled along.
O my mother's fair glory!   O Æther, enringing
All eyes with the sweet common light of thy bringing!
      Dost see how I suffer this wrong?

A LAMENT FOR ADONIS.

FROM THE GREEK OF BION.

A LAMENT FOR ADONIS.

FROM BION.

—◆—

I.

I MOURN for Adonis—Adonis is dead,
　Fair Adonis is dead and the Loves are lamenting.
Sleep, Cypris, no more on thy purple-strewed bed:
　Arise, wretch stoled in black; beat thy breast un-
　　relenting,
And shriek to the worlds, 'Fair Adonis is dead.'

II.

I mourn for Adonis—the Loves are lamenting.
　He lies on the hills in his beauty and death;
The white tusk of a boar has transpierced his white
　　thigh.
　Cytherea grows mad at his thin gasping breath,
While the black blood drips down on the pale ivory,
　And his eyeballs lie quenched with the weight of his
　　brows,
The rose fades from his lips, and upon them just parted
　The kiss dies the goddess consents not to lose.

Though the kiss of the Dead cannot make her glad-
        hearted:
  He knows not who kisses him dead in the dews.

III.

I mourn for Adonis—the Loves are lamenting.
  Deep, deep in the thigh is Adonis's wound,
But a deeper, is Cypris's bosom presenting.
  The youth lieth dead while his dogs howl around,
And the nymphs weep aloud from the mists of the hill,
  And the poor Aphrodité, with tresses unbound,
All dishevelled, unsandaled, shrieks mournful and shrill
    Through the dusk of the groves. The thorns, tearing
        her feet,
Gather up the red flower of her blood which is holy,
  Each footstep she takes; and the valleys repeat
The sharp cry she utters and draw it out slowly.
  She calls on her spouse, her Assyrian, on him
Her own youth, while the dark blood spreads over his
    body,
  The chest taking hue from the gash in the limb,
And the bosom once ivory, turning to ruddy.

IV.

Ah, ah, Cytherea! the Loves are lamenting.
  She lost her fair spouse and so lost her fair smile:
When he lived she was fair, by the whole world's con-
    senting,
  Whose fairness is dead with him: woe worth the while!

All the mountains above and the oaklands below
    Murmur, ah, ah Adonis! the streams overflow
Aphrodité's deep wail; river-fountains in pity
    Weep soft in the hills, and the flowers as they blow
Redden outward with sorrow, while all hear her go
    With the song of her sadness through mountain and
        city.

v.

Ah, ah, Cytherea! Adonis is dead,
    Fair Adonis is dead—Echo answers, Adonis!
Who weeps not for Cypris, when bowing her head
    She stares at the wound where it gapes and astonies?
—When, ah, ah!—she saw how the blood ran away
    And empurpled the thigh, and, with wild hands flung
        out,
Said with sobs. 'Stay, Adonis! unhappy one, stay,
    ' Let me feel thee once more, let me ring thee about
With the clasp of my arms, and press kiss into kiss!
    Wait a little, Adonis, and kiss me again,
For the last time, beloved,—and but so much of this
    That the kiss may learn life from the warmth of the
        strain!
—Till thy breath shall exude from thy soul to my mouth,
    To my heart, and, the love-charm I once more re-
        ceiving,
May drink thy love in it and keep of a truth
    That one kiss in the place of Adonis the living.

Thou fliest me, mournful one, fliest me far,
    My Adonis, and seekest the Acheron portal,—
To Hell's cruel King goest down with a scar,
    While I weep and live on like a wretched immortal,
And follow no step! O Persephoné, take him,
    My husband!—thou'rt better and brighter than I,
So all beauty flows down to thee: *I* cannot make him
    Look up at my grief; there's despair in my cry,
Since I wail for Adonis who died to me—died to me—
    Then, I fear *thee!*—Art thou dead, my Adored?
Passion ends like a dream in the sleep that's denied to
      me,
    Cypris is widowed, the Loves seek their lord
All the house through in vain. Charm of cestus has
      ceased
    With thy clasp! O too bold in the hunt past pre-
      venting,
Ay, mad, thou so fair, to have strife with a beast!'
    Thus the goddess wailed on—and the Loves are
      lamenting.

VI.

Ah, ah, Cytherea! Adonis is dead.
She wept tear after tear with the blood which was
    shed,
And both turned into flowers for the earth's garden-
    close,
Her tears, to the wind-flower; his blood, to the rose.

VII.

I mourn for Adonis—Adonis is dead.

Weep no more in the woods, Cytherea, thy lover!
So, well: make a place for his corse in thy bed,
   With the purples thou sleepest in, under and over.
He's fair though a corse—a fair corse, like a sleeper.
   Lay him soft in the silks he had pleasure to fold
When, beside thee at night, holy dreams deep and
      deeper
   Enclosed his young life on the couch made of gold.
Love him still, poor Adonis; cast on him together
   The crowns and the flowers: since he died from the
      place,
Why, let all die with him; let the blossoms go wither,
   Rain myrtles and olive-buds down on his face.
Rain the myrrh down, let all that is best fall a-pining,
   Since the myrrh of his life from thy keeping is
      swept.
Pale he lay, thine Adonis, in purples reclining;
   The Loves raised their voices around him and wept.
They have shorn their bright curls off to cast on Adonis;
One treads on his bow,—on his arrows, another,—
One breaks up a well-feathered quiver, and one is
   Bent low at a sandal, untying the strings,
   And one carries the vases of gold from the springs,
While one washes the wound,—and behind them a
      brother
   Fans down on the body sweet air with his wings.

VIII.

Cytherea herself now the Loves are lamenting.
  Each torch at the door Hymenæus blew out;
And, the marriage-wreath dropping its leaves as re-
      penting,
  No more ' Hymen, Hymen,' is chanted about,
But the *ai ai* instead—' ai alas' is begun
  For Adonis, and then follows ' ai Hymenæus!'
The Graces are weeping for Cinyris' son,
  Sobbing low each to each, ' His fair eyes cannot
      see us!'
Their wail strikes more shrill than the sadder Dioné's.
The Fates mourn aloud for Adonis, Adonis,
Deep chanting; he hears not a word that they say:
  He *would* hear, but Persephoné has him in keeping.
—Cease moan, Cytherea! leave pomps for to-day,
  And weep now when a new year refits thee for
      weeping.

A VISION OF POETS.

O Sacred Essence, lighting me this hour,
How may I lightly stile thy great power?
Echo.   Power.
　Power! but of whence? under the greenwood spraye?
　Or liv'st in Heaven? saye.
Echo.   In Heavens aye.
　In Heavens aye! tell, may I it obtayne
　By alms, by fasting, prayer,—by paine?
Echo.   By paine.
　Show me the paine, it shall be undergone:
　I to mine end will still go on.
Echo.   Go on.

A VISION OF POETS.

—◆—

A POET could not sleep aright,
For his soul kept up too much light
Under his eyelids for the night.

And thus he rose disquieted
With sweet rhymes ringing through his head,
And in the forest wanderëd

Where, sloping up the darkest glades,
The moon had drawn long colonnades
Upon whose floor the verdure fades

To a faint silver, pavement fair
The antique wood-nymphs scarce would dare
To foot-print o'er, had such been there,

And rather sit by breathlessly,
With fear in their large eyes, to see
The consecrated sight.   But HE

The poet who, with spirit-kiss
Familiar, had long claimed for his
Whatever earthly beauty is,

Who also in his spirit bore
A beauty passing the earth's store,
Walked calmly onward evermore.

His aimless thoughts in metre went,
Like a babe's hand without intent
Drawn down a seven-stringed instrument:

Nor jarred it with his humour as,
With a faint stirring of the grass.
An apparition fair did pass.

He might have feared another time,
But all things fair and strange did chime
With his thoughts then, as rhyme to rhyme.

An angel had not startled him,
Alighted from heaven's burning rim
To breathe from glory in the Dim;

Much less a lady riding slow
Upon a palfrey white as snow,
And smooth as a snow-cloud could go.

Full upon his she turned her face,
'What ho, sir poet! dost thou pace
Our woods at night in ghostly chace

'Of some fair Dryad of old tales
Who chants between the nightingales
And over sleep by song prevails?'

She smiled; but he could see arise
Her soul from far adown her eyes,
Prepared as if for sacrifice.

She looked a queen who seemeth gay
From royal grace alone. 'Now, nay,'
He answered, 'slumber passed away

'Compelled by instincts in my head
That I should see to-night, instead
Of a fair nymph, some fairer Dread.'

She looked up quickly to the sky
And spake: 'The moon's regality
Will hear no praise; She is as I.

'She is in heaven, and I on earth;
This is my kingdom: I come forth
To crown all poets to their worth.'

He brake in with a voice that mourned;
'To their worth, lady? They are scorned
By men they sing for, till inurned.

'To their worth? Beauty in the mind
Leaves the hearth cold, and love-refined
Ambitions make the world unkind.

'The boor who ploughs the daisy down,
The chief whose mortgage of renown,
Fixed upon graves, has bought a crown—

'Both these are happier, more approved
Than poets!—why should I be moved
In saying, both are more beloved?'

'The south can judge not of the north,'
She resumed calmly; 'I come forth
To crown all poets to their worth.

'Yea, verily, to anoint them all
With blessed oils which surely shall
Smell sweeter as the ages fall.'

'As sweet,' the poet said, and rung
A low sad laugh, 'as flowers are, sprung
Out of their graves when they die young;

'As sweet as window-eglantine,
Some bough of which, as they decline,
The hired nurse gathers at their sign:

'As sweet, in short, as perfumed shroud
Which the gay Roman maidens sewed
For English Keats, singing aloud.'

The lady answered, 'Yea, as sweet!
The things thou namest being complete
In fragrance, as I measure it.

'Since sweet the death-clothes and the knell
Of him who having lived, dies well;
And wholly sweet the asphodel

'Stirred softly by that foot of his,
When he treads brave on all that is,
Into the world of souls, from this.

'Since sweet the tears, dropped at the door
Of tearless Death, and even before:
Sweet, consecrated evermore.

'What, dost thou judge it a strange thing
That poets, crowned for vanquishing,
Should bear some dust from out the ring?

'Come on with me, come on with me,
And learn in coming: let me free
Thy spirit into verity.'

She ceased : her palfrey's paces sent
No separate noises as she went;
'Twas a bee's hum, a little spent.

And while the poet seemed to tread
Along the drowsy noise so made,
The forest heaved up overhead

Its billowy foliage through the air,
And the calm stars did far and spare
O'erswim the masses everywhere

Save when the overtopping pines
Did bar their tremulous light with lines
All fixed and black.   Now the moon shines

A broader glory.   You may see
The trees grow rarer presently ;
The air blows up more fresh and free:

Until they come from dark to light,
And from the forest to the sight
Of the large heaven-heart, bare with night,

A fiery throb in every star,
Those burning arteries that are
The conduits of God's life afar.

A wild brown moorland underneath,
And four pools breaking up the heath
With white low gleamings, blank as death.

Beside the first pool, near the wood,
A dead tree in set horror stood,
Peeled and disjointed, stark as rood;

Since thunder-stricken, years ago,
Fixed in the spectral strain and throe
Wherewith it struggled from the blow:

A monumental tree, alone,
That will not bend in storms, nor groan,
But break off sudden like a stone.

Its lifeless shadow lies oblique
Upon the pool where, javelin-like,
The star-rays quiver while they strike.

'Drink,' said the lady, very still—
'Be holy and cold.' He did her will
And drank the starry water chill.

The next pool they came near unto
Was bare of trees; there, only grew
Straight flags, and lilies just a few

Which sullen on the water sate
And leant their faces on the flat,
As weary of the starlight-state.

'Drink,' said the lady, grave and slow—
'*World's use* behoveth thee to know.'
He drank the bitter wave below.

The third pool, girt with thorny bushes
And flaunting weeds and reeds and rushes
That winds sang through in mournful gushes,

Was whitely smeared in many a round
By a slow slime; the starlight swound
Over the ghastly light it found.

'Drink,' said the lady, sad and slow—
'*World's love* behoveth thee to know.'
He looked to her commanding so;

Her brow was troubled but her eye
Struck clear to his soul.   For all reply
He drank the water suddenly,—

Then, with a deathly sickness, passed
Beside the fourth pool and the last,
Where weights of shadow were downcast

From yew and alder and rank trails
Of nightshade clasping the trunk-scales
And flung across the intervals

From yew to yew: who dares to stoop
Where those dank branches overdroop,
Into his heart the chill strikes up,

He hears a silent gliding coil,
The snakes strain hard against the soil,
His foot slips in their slimy oil,

And toads seem crawling on his hand,
And clinging bats but dimly scanned
Full in his face their wings expand.

A paleness took the poet's cheek:
'Must I drink *here?*' he seemed to seek
The lady's will with utterance meek:

'Ay, ay,' she said, 'it so must be;'
(And this time she spake cheerfully)
'Behoves thee know *World's cruelty.*'

He bowed his forehead till his mouth
Curved in the wave, and drank unloth
As if from rivers of the south;

His lips sobbed through the water rank,
His heart paused in him while he drank,
His brain beat heart-like, rose and sank,

And he swooned backward to a dream
Wherein he lay 'twixt gloom and gleam,
With Death and Life at each extreme:

And spiritual thunders, born of soul
Not cloud, did leap from mystic pole
And o'er him roll and counter-roll,

Crushing their echoes reboant
With their own wheels. Did Heaven so grant
His spirit a sign of covenant?

At last came silence. A slow kiss
Did crown his forehead after this;
His eyelids flew back for the bliss—

The lady stood beside his head,
Smiling a thought, with hair dispread;
The moonshine seemed dishevelled

In her sleek tresses manifold
Like Danae's in the rain of old
That dripped with melancholy gold:

But SHE was holy, pale and high
As one who saw an ecstasy
Beyond a foretold agony.

'Rise up!' said she with voice where song
Eddied through speech, 'rise up; be strong;
And learn how right avenges wrong.'

The poet rose up on his feet:
He stood before an altar set
For sacrament with vessels meet

And mystic altar-lights which shine
As if their flames were crystalline
Carved flames that would not shrink or pine.

The altar filled the central place
Of a great church, and toward its face
Long aisles did shoot and interlace

And from it a continuous mist
Of incense (round the edges kissed
By a yellow light of amethyst)

Wound upward slowly and throbbingly,
Cloud within cloud, right silverly,
Cloud above cloud, victoriously,—

Broke full against the archëd roof
And thence refracting eddied off
And floated through the marble woof

Of many a fine-wrought architrave,
Then, poising its white masses brave,
Swept solemnly down aisle and nave

Where now in dark and now in light
The countless columns, glimmering white,
Seemed leading out to the Infinite :

Plunged halfway up the shaft they showed,
In that pale shifting incense-cloud
Which flowed them by and overflowed

Till mist and marble seemed to blend
And the whole temple, at the end,
With its own incense to distend,—

The arches like a giant's bow
To bend and slacken,—and below,
The nichëd saints to come and go :

Alone amid the shifting scene
That central altar stood serene
In its clear steadfast taper-sheen.

Then first, the poet was aware
Of a chief angel standing there
Before that altar, in the glare.

His eyes were dreadful, for you saw
That *they* saw God; his lips and jaw
Grand-made and strong, as Sinai's law

They could enunciate and refrain
From vibratory after-pain,
And his brow's height was sovereign :

On the vast background of his wings
Rises his image, and he flings
From each plumed arc pale glitterings

And fiery flakes (as beateth more
Or less, the angel-heart) before
And round him upon roof and floor,

Edging with fire the shifting fumes,
While at his side 'twixt lights and glooms
The phantasm of an organ booms.

Extending from which instrument
And angel, right and left-way bent,
The poet's sight grew sentient

Of a strange company around
And toward the altar; pale and bound
With bay above the eyes profound.

Deathful their faces were, and yet
The power of life was in them set—
Never forgot nor to forget :

Sublime significance of mouth,
Dilated nostril full of youth,
And forehead royal with the truth.

These faces were not multiplied
Beyond your count, but side by side
Did front the altar, glorified,

Still as a vision, yet exprest
Full as an action—look and geste
Of buried saint in risen rest.

The poet knew them.   Faint and dim
His spirits seemed to sink in him—
Then, like a dolphin, change and swim

The current: these were poets true,
Who died for Beauty as martyrs do
For Truth—the ends being scarcely two.

God's prophets of the Beautiful
These poets were; of iron rule,
The rugged cilix, serge of wool.

Here Homer, with the broad suspense
Of thunderous brows, and lips intense
Of garrulous god-innocence.

There Shakespeare, on whose forehead climb
The crowns o' the world: O eyes sublime
With tears and laughters for all time!

Here Æschylus, the women swooned
To see so awful when he frowned
As the gods did: he standeth crowned.

Euripides, with close and mild
Scholastic lips, that could be wild
And laugh or sob out like a child

Even in the classes. Sophocles,
With that king's-look which down the trees
Followed the dark effigies

Of the lost Theban. Hesiod old,
Who, somewhat blind and deaf and cold,
Cared most for gods and bulls. And bold

Electric Pindar, quick as fear,
With race-dust on his cheeks, and clear
Slant startled eyes that seem to hear

The chariot rounding the last goal,
To hurtle past it in his soul.
And Sappho, with that gloriole

Of ebon hair on calmèd brows—
O poet-woman! none forgoes
The leap, attaining the repose.

Theocritus, with glittering locks
Dropt sideway, as betwixt the rocks
He watched the visionary flocks.

And Aristophanes, who took
The world with mirth, and laughter-struck
The hollow caves of Thought and woke

The infinite echoes hid in each.
And Virgil: shade of Mantuan beech
Did help the shade of bay to reach

And knit around his forehead high :
For his gods wore less majesty
Than his brown bees hummed deathlessly.

Lucretius, nobler than his mood,
Who dropped his plummet down the broad
Deep universe and said 'No God—'

Finding no bottom : he denied
Divinely the divine, and died
Chief poet on the Tiber-side

By grace of God : his face is stern
As one compelled, in spite of scorn,
To teach a truth he would not learn.

And Ossian, dimly seen or guessed ;
Once counted greater than the rest,
When mountain-winds blew out his vest.

And Spenser drooped his dreaming head
(With languid sleep-smile you had said
From his own verse engenderëd)

On Ariosto's, till they ran
Their curls in one : the Italian
Shot nimbler heat of bolder man

From his fine lids.   And Dante stern
And sweet, whose spirit was an urn
For wine and milk poured out in turn.

Hard-souled Alfieri; and fancy-willed
Boiardo, who with laughter filled
The pauses of the jostled shield.

And Berni, with a hand stretched out
To sleek that storm.   And, not without
The wreath he died in and the doubt

He died by, Tasso, bard and lover,
Whose visions were too thin to cover
The face of a false woman over.

And soft Racine ; and grave Corneille,
The orator of rhymes, whose wail
Scarce shook his purple.   And Petrarch pale,

From whose brainlighted heart were thrown
A thousand thoughts beneath the sun,
Each lucid with the name of One.

And Camoens, with that look he had,
Compelling India's Genius sad
From the wave through the Lusiad,—

The murmurs of the storm-cape ocean
Indrawn in vibrative emotion
Along the verse.   And, while devotion

In his wild eyes fantastic shone
Under the tonsure blown upon
By airs celestial, Calderon.

And bold De Vega, who breathed quick
Verse after verse, till death's old trick
Put pause to life and rhetorick.

And Goethe, with that reaching eye
His soul reached out from, far and high,
And fell from inner entity.

And Schiller, with heroic front
Worthy of Plutarch's kiss upon 't,
Too large for wreath of modern wont.

And Chaucer, with his infantine
Familiar clasp of things divine;
That mark upon his lip is wine.

Here, Milton's eyes strike piercing-dim :
The shapes of suns and stars did swim
Like clouds from them, and granted him

God for sole vision. Cowley, there,
Whose active fancy debonair
Drew straws like amber—foul to fair.

Drayton and Browne, with smiles they drew
From outward nature, still kept new
From their own inward nature true.

And Marlowe, Webster, Fletcher, Ben,
Whose fire-hearts sowed our furrows when
The world was worthy of such men.

And Burns, with pungent passionings
Set in his eyes: deep lyric springs
Are of the fire-mount's issuings.

And Shelley, in his white ideal,
All statue-blind. And Keats the real
Adonis with the hymeneal

Fresh vernal buds half sunk between
His youthful curls, kissed straight and sheen
In his Rome-grave, by Venus queen.

And poor, proud Byron, sad as grave
And salt as life; forlornly brave,
And quivering with the dart he drave.

And visionary Coleridge, who
Did sweep his thoughts as angels do
Their wings with cadence up the Blue.

These poets faced (and many more)
The lighted altar looming o'er
The clouds of incense dim and hoar:

And all their faces, in the lull
Of natural things, looked wonderful
With life and death and deathless rule.

All, still as stone and yet intense;
As if by spirit's vehemence
That stone were carved and not by sense.

But where the heart of each should beat,
There seemed a wound instead of it,
From whence the blood dropped to their feet

Drop after drop—dropped heavily
As century follows century
Into the deep eternity.

Then said the lady—and her word
Came distant, as wide waves were stirred
Between her and the ear that heard,

' *World's use* is cold, *world's love* is vain,
World's cruelty is bitter bane,
But pain is not the fruit of pain.

' Harken, O poet, whom I led
From the dark wood: dismissing dread,
Now hear this angel in my stead.

' His organ's clavier strikes along
These poets' hearts, sonorous, strong,
They gave him without count of wrong,—

' A diapason whence to guide
Up to God's feet, from these who died,
An anthem fully glorified—

' Whereat God's blessing, IBARAK (יברך)
Breathes back this music, folds it back
About the earth in vapoury rack,

' And men walk in it, crying ' Lo
' The world is wider, and we know
' The very heavens look brighter so:

' ' The stars move statelier round the edge
' Of the silver spheres, and give in pledge
' Their light for nobler privilege:

'' No little flower but joys or grieves,
' Full life is rustling in the sheaves,
' Full spirit sweeps the forest-leaves.'

' So works this music on the earth,
God so admits it, sends it forth
To add another worth to worth—

' A new creation-bloom that rounds
The old creation and expounds
His Beautiful in tuneful sounds.

' Now harken!'   Then the poet gazed
Upon the angel glorious-faced
Whose hand, majestically raised,

Floated across the organ-keys,
Like a pale moon o'er murmuring seas,
With no touch but with influences:

Then rose and fell (with swell and swound
Of shapeless noises wandering round
A concord which at last they found)

Those mystic keys: the tones were mixed,
Dim, faint, and thrilled and throbbed betwixt
The incomplete and the unfixed :

And therein mighty minds were heard
In mighty musings, inly stirred,
And struggling outward for a word:

Until these surges, having run
This way and that, gave out as one
An Aphroditè of sweet tune,

A Harmony that, finding vent,
Upward in grand ascension went,
Winged to a heavenly argument,

Up, upward like a saint who strips
The shroud back from his eyes and lips,
And rises in apocalypse:

A harmony sublime and plain,
Which cleft (as flying swan, the rain,—
Throwing the drops off with a strain

Of her white wing) those undertones
Of perplext chords, and soared at once
And struck out from the starry thrones

Their several silver octaves as
It passed to God.   The music was
Of divine stature; strong to pass:

And those who heard it, understood
Something of life in spirit and blood,
Something of nature's fair and good:

And while it sounded, those great souls
Did thrill as racers at the goals
And burn in all their aureoles;

But she the lady, as vapour-bound,
Stood calmly in the joy of sound,
Like Nature with the showers around:

And when it ceased, the blood which fell
Again, alone grew audible,
Tolling the silence as a bell.

The sovran angel lifted high
His hand, and spake out sovranly:
'Tried poets, hearken and reply!

'Give me true answers.   If we grant
That not to suffer, is to want
The conscience of the jubilant,—

'If ignorance of anguish is
But ignorance, and mortals miss
Far prospects, by a level bliss,—

' If, as two colours must be viewed
In a visible image, mortals should
Need good and evil, to see good,—

' If to speak nobly, comprehends
' To feel profoundly,—if the ends
Of power and suffering, Nature blends,—

' If poets on the tripod must
Writhe like the Pythian to make just
Their oracles and merit trust,—

' If every vatic word that sweeps
To change the world must pale their lips
And leave their own souls in eclipse,—

' If to search deep the universe
Must pierce the searcher with the curse,
Because that bolt (in man's reverse)

' Was shot to the heart o' the wood and lies
Wedged deepest in the best,—if eyes
That look for visions and surprise

' From influent angels, must shut down
Their eyelids first to sun and moon,
The head asleep upon a stone,—

'If ONE who did redeem you back,
By His own loss, from final wrack,
Did consecrate by touch and track

'Those temporal sorrows till the taste
Of brackish waters of the waste
Is salt with tears He dropt too fast,—

'If all the crowns of earth must wound
With prickings of the thorns He found,—
If saddest sighs swell sweetest sound,—

'What say ye unto this?—refuse
This baptism in salt water?—choose
Calm breasts, mute lips, and labour loose?

'Or, O ye gifted givers! ye
Who give your liberal hearts to me
To make the world this harmony,

' Are ye resigned that they be spent
To such world's help?'
                                The Spirits bent
Their awful brows and said ' Content.'

Content! it sounded like *amen*
Said by a choir of mourning men ;
An affirmation full of pain

And patience,—ay, of glorying
And adoration, as a king
Might seal an oath for governing.

Then said the angel—and his face
Lightened abroad until the place
Grew larger for a moment's space,—

The long aisles flashing out in light,
And nave and transept, columns white
And arches crossed, being clear to sight

As if the roof were off and all
Stood in the noon-sun,—' Lo, I call
To other hearts as liberal.

' This pedal strikes out in the air :
My instrument has room to bear
Still fuller strains and perfecter.

' Herein is room, and shall be room
While Time lasts, for new hearts to come
Consummating while they consume.

' What living man will bring a gift
Of his own heart and help to lift
The tune ?—The race is to the swift.'

So asxed the angel.   Straight the while,
A company came up the aisle
With measured step and sorted smile;

Cleaving the incense-clouds that rise,
With winking unaccustomed eyes
And love-locks smelling sweet of spice.

One bore his head above the rest
As if the world were dispossessed,
And one did pillow chin on breast,

Right languid, an as he should faint;
One shook his curls across his paint
And moralized on worldly taint;

One, slanting up his face, did wink
The salt rheum to the eyelid's brink,
To think—O gods! or—not to think.

Some trod out stealthily and slow,
As if the sun would fall in snow
If they walked to instead of fro;

And some, with conscious ambling free,
Did shake their bells right daintily
On hand and foot, for harmony;

And some, composing sudden sighs
In attitudes of point-device,
Rehearsed impromptu agonies.

And when this company drew near
The spirits crowned, it might appear
Submitted to a ghastly fear;

As a sane eye in master-passion
Constrains a maniac to the fashion
Of hideous maniac imitation

In the least geste—the dropping low
O' the lid, the wrinkling of the brow,
Exaggerate with mock and mow,—

So mastered was that company
By the crowned vision utterly,
Swayed to a maniac mockery.

One dulled his eyeballs, as they ached
With Homer's forehead, though he lacked
An inch of any; and one racked

His lower lip with restless tooth,
As Pindar's rushing words forsooth
Were pent behind it; one his smooth

Pink cheeks, did rumple passionate
Like Æschylus, and tried to prate
On trolling tongue of fate and fate;

One set her eyes like Sappho's—or
Any light woman's; one forbore
Like Dante, or any man as poor

In mirth, to let a smile undo
His hard-shut lips; and one that drew
Sour humours from his mother, blew

His sunken cheeks out to the size
Of most unnatural jollities,
Because Anacreon looked jest-wise;

So with the rest: it was a sight
A great world-laughter would require,
Or great world-wrath, with equal right.

Out came a speaker from that crowd
To speak for all, in sleek and proud
Exordial periods, while he bowed

His knee before the angel—'Thus,
O angel who hast called for us,
We bring thee service emulous,

' Fit service from sufficient soul,
Hand-service to receive world's dole,
Lip-service in world's ear to roll

' Adjusted concords soft enow
To hear the wine-cups passing, through,
And not too grave to spoil the show :

' Thou, certes, when thou askest more,
O sapient angel, leanest o'er
The window-sill of metaphor.

' To give our hearts up ? fie ! that rage
Barbaric antedates the age ;
It is not done on any stage.

' Because your scald or gleeman went
With seven or nine-stringed instrument
Upon his back,—must ours be bent ?

' We are not pilgrims, by your leave ;
No, nor yet martyrs ; if we grieve,
It is to rhyme to—summer eve :

' And if we labour, it shall be
As suiteth best with our degree,
In after-dinner reverie.'

More yet that speaker would have said,
Poising between his smiles fair-fed
Each separate phrase till finishēd;

But all the foreheads of those born
And dead true poets flashed with scorn
Betwixt the bay leaves round them worn,

Ay, jetted such brave fire that they,
The new-come, shrank and paled away
Like leaden ashes when the day

Strikes on the hearth.   A spirit-blast,
A presence known by power, at last
Took them up mutely: they had passed.

And he our pilgrim-poet saw
Only their places, in deep awe,
What time the angel's smile did draw

His gazing upward.   Smiling on,
The angel in the angel shone,
Revealing glory in benison;

Till, ripened in the light which shut
The poet in, his spirit mute
Dropped sudden as a perfect fruit:

He fell before the angel's feet,
Saying, 'If what is true is sweet,
In something I may compass it:

'For, where my worthiness is poor,
My will stands richly at the door
To pay shortcomings evermore.

'Accept me therefore: not for price
And not for pride my sacrifice
Is tendered, for my soul is nice

'And will beat down those dusty seeds
Of bearded corn if she succeeds
In soaring while the covey feeds.

'I soar, I am drawn up like the lark
To its white cloud: so high my mark.
Albeit my wing is small and dark.

'I ask no wages, seek no fame:
Sew me, for shroud round face and name,
God's banner of the oriflamme.

'I only would have leave to loose
(In tears and blood if so He choose)
Mine inward music out to use;

'I only would be spent—in pain
And loss, perchance, but not in vain—
Upon the sweetness of that strain;

'Only project beyond the bound
Of mine own life, so lost and found,
My voice and live on in its sound;

'Only embrace and be embraced
By fiery ends, whereby to waste,
And light God's future with my past.'

The angel's smile grew more divine,
The mortal speaking; ay, its shine
Swelled fuller, like a choir-note fine,

Till the broad glory round his brow
Did vibrate with the light below;
But what he said, I do not know.

Nor know I if the man who prayed,
Rose up accepted, unforbade,
From the church-floor where he was laid;

Nor if a listening life did run
Through the king-poets, one by one
Rejoicing in a worthy son:

My soul, which might have seen, grew blind
By what it looked on : I can find
No certain count of things behind.

I saw alone, dim, white and grand
As in a dream, the angel's hand
Stretched forth in gesture of command

Straight through the haze.   And so, as erst,
A strain more noble than the first
Mused in the organ, and outburst :

With giant march from floor to roof
Rose the full notes, now parted off
In pauses massively aloof

Like measured thunders, now rejoined
In concords of mysterious kind
Which fused together sense and mind,

Now flashing sharp on sharp along
Exultant in a mounting throng,
Now dying off to a low song

Fed upon minors, wavelike sounds
Re-eddying into silver rounds,
Enlarging liberty with bounds :

And every rhythm that seemed to close
Survived in confluent underflows
Symphonious with the next that rose.

Thus the whole strain being multiplied
And greatened, with its glorified
Wings shot abroad from side to side,

Waved backward (as a wind might wave
A Brocken mist and with as brave
Wild roaring) arch and architrave,

Aisle, transept, column, marble wall,—
Then swelling outward, prodigal
Of aspiration beyond thrall,

Soared, and drew up with it the whole
Of this said vision, as a soul
Is raised by a thought.   And as a scroll

Of bright devices is unrolled
Still upward with a gradual gold,
So rose the vision manifold,

Angel and organ, and the round
Of spirits, solemnized and crowned;
While the freed clouds of incense wound

Ascending, following in their track,
And glimmering faintly like the rack
O' the moon in her own light cast back.

And as that solemn dream withdrew,
The lady's kiss did fall anew
Cold on the poet's brow as dew.

And that same kiss which bound him first
Beyond the senses, now reversed
Its own law and most subtly pierced

His spirit with the sense of things
Sensual and present.   Vanishings
Of glory with Æolian wings

Struck him and passed : the lady's face
Did melt back in the chrysopras
Of the orient morning sky that was

Yet clear of lark and there and so
She melted as a star might do,
Still smiling as she melted slow :

Smiling so slow, he seemed to see
Her smile the last thing, gloriously
Beyond her, far as memory.

Then he looked round : he was alone.
He lay before the breaking sun,
As Jacob at the Bethel stone.

And thought's entangled skein being wound,
He knew the moorland of his swound,
And the pale pools that smeared the ground;

The far wood-pines like offing ships;
The fourth pool's yew anear him drips,
World's cruelty attaints his lips,

And still he tastes it, bitter still;
Through all that glorious possible
He had the sight of present ill.

Yet rising calmly up and slowly
With such a cheer as scorneth folly,
A mild delightsome melancholy,

He journeyed homeward through the wood
And prayed along the solitude
Betwixt the pines, 'O God, my God!'

The golden morning's open flowings
Did sway the trees to murmurous bowings,
In metric chant of blessed poems.

And passing homeward through the wood
He prayed along the solitude,
' Thou, Poet-God, art great and good !

' And though we must have, and have had
Right reason to be earthly sad,
' Thou, Poet-God, art great and glad !'

CONCLUSION.

Life treads on life, and heart on heart;
We press too close in church and mart
To keep a dream or grave apart :

And I was 'ware of walking down
That same green forest where had gone
The poet-pilgrim.   One by one

I traced his footsteps.   From the east
A red and tender radiance pressed
Through the near trees, until I guessed

The sun behind shone full and round ;
While up the leafiness profound
A wind scarce old enough for sound

Stood ready to blow on me when
I turned that way, and now and then
The birds sang and brake off again

To shake their pretty feathers dry
Of the dew sliding droppingly
From the leaf-edges and apply

Back to their song: 'twixt dew and bird
So sweet a silence ministered,
God seemed to use it for a word,

Yet morning souls did leap and run
In all things, as the least had won
A joyous insight of the sun,

And no one looking round the wood
Could help confessing as he stood,
This Poet-God is glad and good.

But hark! a distant sound that grows,
A heaving, sinking of the boughs,
A rustling murmur, not of those,

A breezy noise which is not breeze!
And white-clad children by degrees
Steal out in troops among the trees,

Fair little children morning-bright,
With faces grave yet soft to sight,
Expressive of restrained delight.

Some plucked the palm-boughs within reach,
And others leapt up high to catch
The upper boughs and shake from each

A rain of dew till, wetted so,
The child who held the branch let go
And it swang backward with a flow

Of faster drippings.   Then I knew
The children laughed; but the laugh flew
From its own chirrup as might do

A frightened song-bird; and a child
Who seemed the chief said very mild,
· Hush! keep this morning undefiled.'

His eyes rebuked them from calm spheres;
His soul upon his brow appears
In waiting for more holy years.

I called the child to me, and said,
' What are your palms for?'   ' To be spread'
He answered, ' on a poet dead.

'The poet died last month, and now
The world which had been somewhat slow
In honouring his living brow,

'Commands the palms; they must be strown
On his new marble very soon,
In a procession of the town.'

I sighed and said, 'Did he foresee
Any such honour?'   'Verily
I cannot tell you,' answered he.

'But this I know, I fain would lay
My own head down, another day,
As *he* did,—with the fame away.

'A lily, a friend's hand had plucked,
Lay by his death-bed, which he looked
As deep down as a bee had sucked,

'Then, turning to the lattice, gazed
O'er hill and river and upraised
His eyes illumined and amazed

'With the world's beauty, up to God,
Re-offering on their iris broad
The images of things bestowed

' By the chief Poet. ' God !' he cried,
" Be praised for anguish which has tried,
For beauty which has satisfied :

" For this world's presence half within
And half without me—thought and scene—
This sense of Being and Having been.

" I thank Thee that my soul hath room
For Thy grand world : both guests may come—
Beauty, to soul—Body, to tomb.

" I am content to be so weak :
Put strength into the words I speak,
And I am strong in what I seek.

" I am content to be so bare
Before the archers, everywhere
My wounds being stroked by heavenly air.

" I laid my soul before Thy feet
That images of fair and sweet
Should walk to other men on it.

" I am content to feel the step
Of each pure image : let those keep
To mandragore who care to sleep.

"'I am content to touch the brink
Of the other goblet and I think
My bitter drink a wholesome drink.

"Because my portion was assigned
Wholesome and bitter, Thou art kind,
And I am blessed to my mind.

"Gifted for giving, I receive
The maythorn and its scent outgive:
I grieve not that I once did grieve.

"In my large joy of sight and touch
Beyond what others count for such,
I am content to suffer much.

"*I know*—is all the mourner saith,
Knowledge by suffering entereth,
And Life is perfected by Death.''

The child spake nobly: strange to hear,
His infantine soft accents clear
Charged with high meanings, did appear;

And fair to see, his form and face
Winged out with whiteness and pure grace
From the green darkness of the place.

Behind his head a palm-tree grew ;
An orient beam which pierced it through
Transversely on his forehead drew

The figure of a palm-branch brown
Traced on its brightness up and down
In fine fair lines,—a shadow-crown :

Guido might paint his angels so—
A little angel, taught to go
With holy words to saints below—

Such innocence of action yet
Significance of object met
In his whole bearing strong and sweet.

And all the children, the whole band,
Did round in rosy reverence stand,
Each with a palm-bough in his hand.

' And so he died,' I whispered.   ' Nay,
Not so,' the childish voice did say,
' That poet turned him first to pray

' In silence, and God heard the rest
'Twixt the sun's footsteps down the west.
Then he called one who loved him best,

Yea, he called softly through the room
(His voice was weak yet tender)—'Come,'
He said, ' come nearer!   Let the bloom

'' Of Life grow over, undenied,
This bridge of Death, which is not wide—
I shall be soon at the other side.

'' Come, kiss me!'   So the one in truth
Who loved him best,—in love, not ruth,
Bowed down and kissed him mouth to mouth:

' And in that kiss of love was won
Life's manumission.   All was done :
The mouth that kissed last, kissed *alone.*

' But in the former, confluent kiss,
The same was sealed, I think, by His,
To words of truth and uprightness.'

The child's voice trembled, his lips shook
Like a rose leaning o'er a brook,
Which vibrates though it is not struck.

' And who,' I asked, a little moved
Yet curious-eyed, ' was this that loved
And kissed him last, as it behoved ? '

'*I*,' softly said the child ; and then,
'*I*,' said he louder, once again :
' His son, my rank is among men :

' And now that men exalt his name
I come to gather palms with them,
That holy love may hallow fame.

' He did not die alone, nor should
His memory live so, 'mid these rude
World-praisers—a worse solitude.

' Me, a voice calleth to that tomb
Where these are strewing branch and bloom,
Saying, ' Come nearer :' and I come.

' Glory to God !' resumëd he,
And his eyes smiled for victory
O'er their own tears which I could see

Fallen on the palm, down cheek and chin—
' That poet now has entered in
The place of rest which is not sin.

' And while he rests, his songs in troops
Walk up and down our earthly slopes,
Companioned by diviner hopes.'

' But *thou*,' I murmured to engage
The child's speech farther—' hast an age
Too tender for this orphanage.'

' Glory to God—to God!' he saith,
' KNOWLEDGE BY SUFFERING ENTERETH,
AND LIFE IS PERFECTED BY DEATH.'

THE POET'S VOW.

—— O be wiser thou
Instructed that true knowledge leads to love.

WORDSWORTH

THE POET'S VOW.

I.

Eve is a twofold mystery;
 The stillness Earth doth keep,
The motion wherewith human hearts
 Do each to either leap
As if all souls between the poles
 Felt ' Parting comes in sleep.'

II.

The rowers lift their oars to view
 Each other in the sea;
The landsmen watch the rocking boats
 In a pleasant company;
While up the hill go gladlier still
 Dear friends by two and three.

III.

The peasant's wife hath looked without
  Her cottage door and smiled,
For there the peasant drops his spade
  To clasp his youngest child
Which hath no speech, but its hand can reach
  And stroke his forehead mild.

IV.

A poet sate that eventide
  Within his hall alone,
As silent as its ancient lords
  In the coffined place of stone,
When the bat hath shrunk from the praying monk,
  And the praying monk is gone.

V.

Nor wore the dead a stiller face
  Beneath the cerement's roll:
His lips refusing out in words
  Their mystic thoughts to dole,
His steadfast eye burnt inwardly,
  As burning out his soul.

VI.

You would not think that brow could e'er
  Ungentle moods express,
Yet seemed it, in this troubled world,
  Too calm for gentleness,
When the very star that shines from far
  Shines trembling ne'ertheless.

VII.

It lacked, all need, the softening light
    Which other brows supply:
We should conjoin the scathëd trunks
    Of our humanity,
That each leafless spray entwining may
    Look softer 'gainst the sky.

VIII.

None gazed within the poet's face,
    The poet gazed in none;
He threw a lonely shadow straight
    Before the moon and sun,
Affronting nature's heaven-dwelling creatures
    With wrong to nature done:

IX.

Because this poet daringly,
    —The nature at his heart,
And that quick tune along his veins
    He could not change by art,—
Had vowed his blood of brotherhood
    To a stagnant place apart.

X.

He did not vow in fear, or wrath,
    Or grief's fantastic whim,
But, weights and shows of sensual things
    Too closely crossing him,
On his soul's eyelid the pressure slid
    And made its vision dim.

XI.

And darkening in the dark he strove
   'Twixt earth and sea and sky
To lose in shadow, wave and cloud,
   His brother's haunting cry:
The winds were welcome as they swept,
God's five-day work he would accept,
   But let the rest go by.

XII.

He cried, ' O touching, patient Earth
   That weepest in thy glee,
Whom God created very good,
   And very mournful, we !
Thy voice of moan doth reach His throne,
   As Abel's rose from thee.

XIII.

' Poor crystal sky with stars astray !
   Mad winds that howling go
From east to west ! perplexëd seas
   That stagger from their blow !
O motion wild ! O wave defiled !
   Our curse hath made you so.

XIV.

' *We !* and *our* curse ! do *I* partake
   The desiccating sin ?
Have *I* the apple at my lips ?
   The money-lust within ?
Do *I* human stand with the wounding hand,
   To the blasting heart akin ?

xv.

'Thou solemn pathos of all things,
  For solemn joy designed!
Behold, submissive to your cause,
  An holy wrath I find
And, for your sake, the bondage break
  That knits me to my kind.

xvi.

' Hear me forswear man's sympathies
  His pleasant yea and no,
His riot on the piteous earth
  Whereon his thistles grow,
His changing love—with stars above,
  His pride—with graves below.

xvii.

' Hear me forswear his roof by night,
  His bread and salt by day,
His talkings at the wood-fire hearth,
  His greetings by the way,
His answering looks, his systemed books,
  All man, for aye and aye.

xviii.

' That so my purged, once human heart
  From all the human rent,
May gather strength to pledge and drink
  Your wine of wonderment,
While you pardon me all blessingly
  The woe mine Adam sent.

XIX.

'And I shall feel your unseen looks
　Innumerous, constant, deep
And soft as haunted Adam once,
　Though sadder, round me creep.—
As slumbering men have mystic ken
　Of watchers on their sleep.

XX.

'And ever, when 1 lift my brow
　At evening to the sun,
No voice of woman or of child
　Recording ' Day is done.'
Your silences shall a love express,
　More deep than such an one.'

PART THE SECOND.

—✦—

I.

THE poet's vow was inly sworn,
  The poet's vow was told.
He shared among his crowding friends
  The silver and the gold,
They clasping bland his gift,—his hand
  In a somewhat slacker hold.

II.

They wended forth, the crowding friends,
  With farewells smooth and kind.
They wended forth, the solaced friends,
  And left but twain behind :
One loved him true as brothers do,
  And one was Rosalind.

III.

He said, 'My friends have wended forth
  With farewells smooth and kind ;
Mine oldest friend, my plighted bride,
  Ye need not stay behind :
Friend, wed my fair bride for my sake,
And let my lands ancestral make
  A dower for Rosalind.

IV.

'And when beside your wassail board
  Ye bless your social lot,
I charge you that the giver be
  In all his gifts forgot,
Or alone of all his words recall
  The last,—Lament me not.'

V.

She looked upon him silently
  With her large, doubting eyes,
Like a child that never knew but love
  Whom words of wrath surprise,
Till the rose did break from either cheek
  And the sudden tears did rise.

VI.

She looked upon him mournfully,
  While her large eyes were grown
Yet larger with the steady tears,
  Till, all his purpose known,
She turnëd slow, as she would go—
  The tears were shaken down.

VII.

She turnëd slow, as she would go,
  Then quickly turned again,
And gazing in his face to seek
  Some little touch of pain,
'I thought,' she said,—but shook her head,—
  She tried that speech in vain.

VIII.

' I thought—but I am half a child
  And very sage art thou—
The teachings of the heaven and earth
  Should keep us soft and low .
They have drawn *my* tears in early years,
  Or ere I wept—as now.

IX.

' But now that in thy face I read
  Their cruel homily,
Before their beauty I would fain
  Untouched, unsoftened be,—
If I indeed could look on even
The senseless, loveless earth and heaven
  As thou canst look on me !

X.

' And couldest thou as coldly view
  Thy childhood's far abode,
Where little feet kept time with thine
  Along the dewy sod,
And thy mother's look from holy book
  Rose like a thought of God ?

XI.

' O brother,—called so, ere her last
  Betrothing words were said !
O fellow-watcher in her room,
  With hushëd voice and tread !
Rememberest thou how, hand in hand.
O friend, O lover, we did stand,
  And knew that she was dead ?

XII.

'I will not live Sir Roland's bride,
    That dower I will not hold;
I tread below my feet that go,
    These parchments bought and sold:
The tears I weep, are mine to keep,
    And worthier than thy gold.'

XIII.

The poet and Sir Roland stood
    Alone, each turned to each,
Till Roland brake the silence left
    By that soft-throbbing speech—
'Poor heart!' he cried, 'it vainly tried
    The distant heart to reach.

XIV.

'And thou, O distant, sinful heart
    That climbest up so high
To wrap and blind thee with the snows
    That cause to dream and die,
What blessing can, from lips of man,
    Approach thee with his sigh?

XV.

'Ay, what from earth—create for man
    And moaning in his moan?
Ay, what from stars—revealed to man
    And man-named one by one?
Ay, more! what blessing can be given
Where the Spirits seven do show in heaven
    A MAN upon the throne?

XVI.

'A man on earth HE wandered once,
  All meek and undefiled,
And those who loved Him said 'He wept'—
  None ever said He smiled;
Yet there might have been a smile unseen,
When He bowed his holy face, I ween,
  To bless that happy child.

XVII.

'And now HE pleadeth up in heaven
  For our humanities,
Till the ruddy light on seraphs' wings
  In pale emotion dies.
They can better bear their Godhead's glare
Than the pathos of his eyes.

XVIII.

'I will go pray our God to-day
  To teach thee how to scan
His work divine, for human use
  Since earth on axle ran,—
To teach thee to discern as plain
His grief divine, the blood-drop's stain
  He left there, MAN for man.

XIX.

'So, for the blood's sake shed by Him
  Whom angels God declare,
Tears like it, moist and warm with love,
  Thy reverent eyes shall wear
To see i' the face of Adam's race
  The nature God doth share.'

XX.

' I heard,' the poet said, ' thy voice
    As dimly as thy breath :
The sound was like the noise of life
    To one anear his death,—
Or of waves that fail to stir the pale
    Sere leaf they roll beneath.

XXI.

' And still between the sound and me
    White creatures like a mist
Did interfloat confusedly,
    Mysterious shapes unwist :
Across my heart and across my brow
I felt them droop like wreaths of snow,
    To still the pulse they kist.

XXII.

' The castle and its lands are thine—
    The poor's—it shall be done.
Go, *man*, to love ! I go to live
    In Courland hall, alone :
The bats along the ceilings cling,
The lizards in the floors do run,
And storms and years have worn and reft
The stain by human builders left
    In working at the stone.'

PART THE THIRD.

SHOWING HOW THE VOW WAS KEPT.

— ◆ —

I.

He dwelt alone, and sun and moon
   Were witness that he made
Rejection of his humanness
   Until they seemed to fade;
His face did so, for he did grow
   Of his own soul afraid.

II.

The self-poised God may dwell alone
   With inward glorying,
But God's chief angel waiteth for
   A brother's voice, to sing;
And a lonely creature of sinful nature—
   It is an awful thing.

III.

An awful thing that feared itself;
   While many years did roll,
A lonely man, a feeble man,
   A part beneath the whole,
He bore by day, he bore by night
That pressure of God's infinite
   Upon his finite soul.

IV.

The poet at his lattice sate
  And downward lookĕd he.
Three Christians wended by to prayers,
  With mute ones in their ee;
Each turned above a face of love
  And called him to the far chapèlle
With voice more tuneful than its bell:
  But still they wended three.

V.

There journeyed by a bridal pomp,
  A bridegroom and his dame;
He speaketh low for happiness,
  She blusheth red for shame:
But never a tone of benison
  From out the lattice came.

VI.

A little child with inward song,
  No louder noise to dare,
Stood near the wall to see at play
  The lizards green and rare—
Unblessed the while for his childish smile
  Which cometh unaware.

PART THE FOURTH.

SHOWING HOW ROSALIND FARED BY THE KEEPING OF THE VOW.

— ✦ —

I.

In death-sheets lieth Rosalind
  As white and still as they;
And the old nurse that watched her bed
  Rose up with ' Well-a-day!'
And oped the casement to let in
The sun, and that sweet doubtful din
Which droppeth from the grass and bough
Sans wind and bird, none knoweth how—
  To cheer her as she lay.

II.

The old nurse started when she saw
  Her sudden look of woe:
But the quick wan tremblings round her mouth
  In a meek smile did go,
And calm she said, ' When I am dead,
  Dear nurse it shall be so.

III.

'Till then, shut out those sights and sounds,
  And pray God pardon me
That I without this pain no more
  His blessed works can see!

And lean beside me, loving nurse,
That thou mayst hear, ere I am worse
What thy last love should be.'

IV.

The loving nurse leant over her,
 As white she lay beneath;
The old eyes searching, dim with life,
 The young ones dim with death,
To read their look if sound forsook
 The trying, trembling breath.

V.

' When all this feeble breath is done
 And I on bier am laid,
My tresses smoothed for never a feast,
 My body in shroud arrayed,
Uplift each palm in a saintly calm,
 As if that still I prayed.

VI.

' And heap beneath mine head the flowers
 You stoop so low to pull,
The little white flowers from the wood
 Which grow there in the cool,
Which *he* and I, in childhood's games,
Went plucking, knowing not their names,
 And filled thine apron full.

VII.

' Weep not ! *I* weep not.   Death is strong,
   The eyes of Death are dry !
But lay this scroll upon my breast
   When hushed its heavings lie,
And wait awhile for the corpse's smile
   Which shineth presently.

VIII.

' And when it shineth, straightway call
   Thy youngest children dear,
And bid them gently carry me
   All barefaced on the bier ;
But bid them pass my kirkyard grass
   That waveth long anear.

IX.

' And up the bank where I used to sit
   And dream what life would be,
Along the brook with its sunny look
   Akin to living glee,—
O'er the windy hill, through the forest still,
   Let them gently carry me.

X.

' And through the piny forest still,
   And down the open moorland
Round where the sea beats mistily
   And blindly on the foreland ;
And let them chant that hymn I know,
Bearing me soft, bearing me slow,
   To the ancient hall of Courland.

VI.

'And when withal they near the hall,
  In silence let them lay
My bier before the bolted door,
  And leave it for a day :
For I have vowed, though I am proud,
To go there as a guest in shroud,
  And not be turned away.'

XII.

The old nurse looked within her eyes
  Whose mutual look was gone ;
The old nurse stooped upon her mouth,
  Whose answering voice was done ;
And nought she heard, till a little bird
  Upon the casement's woodbine swinging
Broke out into a loud sweet singing
  For joy o' the summer sun :
'Alack ! alack !'—she watched no more,
  With head on knee she wailèd sore,
And the little bird sang o'er and o'er
  For joy o' the summer sun.

PART THE FIFTH.

SHOWING HOW THE VOW WAS BROKEN.

—◆—

I.

THE poet oped his bolted door
  The midnight sky to view;
A spirit-feel was in the air
Which seemed to touch his spirit bare
  Whenever his breath he drew;
And the stars a liquid softness had,
As alone their holiness forbade
  Their falling with the dew.

II.

They shine upon the steadfast hills,
  Upon the swinging tide,
Upon the narrow track of beach
  And the murmuring pebbles pied:
They shine on every lovely place,
They shine upon the corpse's face,
  As *it* were fair beside.

III.

It lay before him, humanlike,
  Yet so unlike a thing!
More awful in its shrouded pomp
  Than any crownëd king:
All calm and cold, as it did hold
  Some secret, glorying.

IV.

A heavier weight than of its clay
　　Clung to his heart and knee :
As if those folded palms could strike
　　He staggered groaningly,
And then o'erhung, without a groan,
The meek close mouth that smiled alone,
　　Whose speech the scroll must be.

———

THE WORDS OF ROSALIND'S SCROLL.

' I LEFT thee last, a child at heart,
　　A woman scarce in years.
I come to thee, a solemn corpse
　　Which neither feels nor fears.
I have no breath to use in sighs ;
They laid the dead-weights on mine eyes
　　To seal them safe from tears.

' Look on me with thine own calm look :
　　I meet it calm as thou.
No look of thine can change *this* smile,
　　Or break thy sinful vow :
I tell thee that my poor scorned heart
Is of thine earth—thine earth, a part :
　　It cannot vex thee now.

'But out, alas! these words are writ
   By a living, loving one
Adown whose cheeks, the proofs of life
   The warm quick tears do run:
Ah, let the unloving corpse control
Thy scorn back from the loving soul
   Whose place of rest is won.

' I have prayed for thee with bursting sobs,
   When passion's course was free;
I have prayed for thee with silent lips,
   In the anguish none could see:
They whispered oft, ' She sleepeth soft'—
   But I only prayed for thee.

' Go to! I pray for thee no more:
   The corpse's tongue is still,
Its folded fingers point to heaven,
   But point there stiff and chill:
No farther wrong, no farther woe
Hath license from the sin below
   Its tranquil heart to thrill.

' I charge thee, by the living's prayer,
   And the dead's silentness,
To wring from out thy soul a cry
   Which God shall hear and bless!

Lest Heaven's own palm droop in my hand,
And pale among the saints I stand,
    A saint companionless.'

---

v.

Bow lower down before the throne,
    Triumphant Rosalind!
He boweth on thy corpse his face,
    And weepeth as the blind :
'Twas a dread sight to see them so,
For the senseless corpse rocked to and fro
    With the wail of his living mind.

vi.

But dreader sight, could such be seen.
    His inward mind did lie,
Whose long-subjected humanness
    Gave out its lion cry,
And fiercely rent its tenement
    In a mortal agony.

vii.

I tell you, friends, had you heard his wail,
    'Twould haunt you in court and mart,
And in merry feast until you set
    Your cup down to depart—
That weeping wild of a reckless child
    From a proud man's broken heart.

VIII.

O broken heart, O broken vow,
    That wore so proud a feature!
God, grasping as a thunderbolt
    The man's rejected nature,
Smote him therewith i' the presence high
Of his so worshipped earth and sky
That looked on all indifferently—
    A wailing human creature.

IX.

A human creature found too weak
    To bear his human pain—
(May Heaven's dear grace have spoken peace
    To his dying heart and brain!)
For when they came at dawn of day
To lift the lady's corpse away,
    Her bier was holding twain.

X.

They dug beneath the kirkyard grass,
    For both one dwelling deep;
To which, when years had mossed the stone,
Sir Roland brought his little son
    To watch the funeral heap:
And when the happy boy would rather
    Turn upward his blithe eyes to see
    The wood-doves nodding from the tree,
'Nay, boy, look downward,' said his father.

'Upon this human dust asleep.
And hold it in thy constant ken
That God's own unity compresses
   (One into one) the human many,
And that his everlastingness is
   The bond which is not loosed by any:
That thou and 1 this law must keep,
   If not in love, in sorrow then,—
   Though smiling not like other men,
Still, like them we must weep.'

THE ROMAUNT OF MARGRET.

Can my affectious find out nothing best,
But still and still remove?

QUARLES.

THE ROMAUNT OF MARGRET.

— ◆ —

I.

I PLANT a tree whose leaf
    The yew-tree leaf will suit:
But when its shade is o'er you laid,
    Turn round and pluck the fruit.
Now reach my harp from off the wall
    Where shines the sun aslant;
The sun may shine and we be cold!
O harken, loving hearts and bold,
    Unto my wild romaunt,
              Margret, Margret.

II.

Sitteth the fair ladye
    Close to the river side
Which runneth on with a merry tone
    Her merry thoughts to guide:
It runneth through the trees,
    It runneth by the hill,
Nathless the lady's thoughts have found
    A way more pleasant still.
              Margret, Margret.

III.

The night is in her hair
    And giveth shade to shade,
And the pale moonlight on her forehead white
    Like a spirit's hand is laid;
Her lips part with a smile
    Instead of speakings done:
I ween, she thinketh of a voice,
    Albeit uttering none.
                    Margret, Margret.

IV.

All little birds do sit
    With heads beneath their wings:
Nature doth seem in a mystic dream,
    Absorbed from her living things:
That dream by that ladye
    Is certes unpartook,
For she looketh to the high cold stars
    With a tender human look.
                    Margret, Margret,

V.

The lady's shadow lies
    Upon the running river;
It lieth no less in its quietness,
    For that which resteth never:
Most like a trusting heart
    Upon a passing faith,

Or as upon the course of life
　The steadfast doom of death.
　　　　Margret, Margret.

VI.

The lady doth not move,
　The lady doth not dream,
Yet she seeth her shade no longer laid
　In rest upon the stream :
It shaketh without wind,
　It parteth from the tide,
It standeth upright in the cleft moonlight,
　It sitteth at her side.
　　　　Margret, Margret.

VII.

Look in its face, ladye,
　And keep thee from thy swound ;
With a spirit bold thy pulses hold
　And hear its voice's sound :
For so will sound thy voice
　When thy face is to the wall,
And such will be thy face, ladye,
　When the maidens work thy pall.
　　　　Margret, Margret.

VIII.

'Am I not like to thee?'
　The voice was calm and low.

And between each word you might have heard
　　The silent forests grow ;
　　　' *The like may sway the like ;*'
　　　By which mysterious law
Mine eyes from thine and my lips from thine
　　　The light and breath may draw.
　　　　　　　Margret, Margret.

　　　　　　　IX.

　　　' My lips do need thy breath,
　　　My lips do need thy smile,
And my pallid eyne, that light in thine
　　　Which met the stars erewhile :
　　　Yet go with light and life
　　　If that thou lovest one
In all the earth who loveth thee
　　　As truly as the sun,
　　　　　　　Margret, Margret.

　　　　　　　X.

　　　Her cheek had waxëd white
　　　Like cloud at fall of snow ;
Then like to one at set of sun,
　　　It waxëd red alsò ;
　　　For love's name maketh bold
　　　As if the loved were near :
And then she sighed the deep long sigh
　　　Which cometh after fear.
　　　　　　　Margret, Margret.

XI.

'Now, sooth, I fear thee not—
    Shall never fear thee now!'
(And a noble sight was the sudden light
    Which lit her lifted brow.)
'Can earth be dry of streams,
    Or hearts of love?' she said;
'Who doubteth love, can know not love:
    He is already dead.'
                    Margret, Margret,

XII.

'I have'... and here her lips
    Some word in pause did keep,
And gave the while a quiet smile
    As if they paused in sleep,—
'I have ... a brother dear,
    A knight of knightly fame!
I broidered him a knightly scarf
    With letters of my name.
                    Margret, Margret.

XIII.

'I fed his grey gosshawk,
    I kissed his fierce bloodhound,
I sate at home when he might come
    And caught his horn's far sound:
I sang him hunter's songs,
    I poured him the red wine,

He looked across the cup and said,
I love thee, sister mine.'
Margret, Margret.

XIV.

IT trembled on the grass
With a low, shadowy laughter ;
The sounding river which rolled, for ever
Stood dumb and stagnant after :
' Brave knight thy brother is !
But better loveth he
Thy chaliced wine than thy chaunted song,
And better both than thee,
Margret, Margret.'

XV.

The lady did not heed
The river's silence while
Her own thoughts still ran at their will.
And calm was still her smile.
' My little sister wears
The look our mother wore :
I smooth her locks with a golden comb,
I bless her evermore.'
Margret, Margret.

XVI.

I gave her my first bird
When first my voice it knew ;

I made her share my posies rare
    And told her where they grew :
I taught her God's dear name
    With prayer and praise to tell, ·
She looked from heaven into my face
    And said, *I love thee well.*'
             Margret, Margret.

XVII.

  IT trembled on the grass
    With a low, shadowy laughter ;
You could see each bird as it woke and stared
    Through the shrivelled foliage after.
  ' Fair child thy sister is !
    But better loveth she
Thy golden comb than thy gathered flowers,
    And better both than thee,
             Margret, Margret.'

XVIII.

  Thy lady did not heed
    The withering on the bough ;
Still calm her smile albeit the while
    A little pale her brow :
  ' I have a father old,
    The lord of ancient halls ;
An hundred friends are in his court
    Yet only me he calls.
             Margret, Margret.

XIX.

'An hundred knights are in his court
 Yet read I by his knee ;
And when forth they go to the tourney show
 I rise not up to see :
 'Tis a weary book to read,
 My tryst's at set of sun,
But loving and dear beneath the stars
 Is his blessing when I've done.'
                    Margret, Margret.

XX.

IT trembled on the grass
 With a low, shadowy laughter ;
And moon and star though bright and far
 Did shrink and darken after.
 'High lord thy father is !
 But better loveth he
His ancient halls than his hundred friends,
 His ancient halls, than thee,
                    Margret, Margret.'

XXI.

The lady did not heed
 That the far stars did fail ;
Still calm her smile, albeit the while . . .
 Nay, but she is not pale !
 'I have more than a friend
 Across the mountains dim :

No other's voice is soft to me,
  Unless it nameth *him.*'
     Margret, Margret.

XXII.

'Though louder beats my heart
  I know his tread again,
And his fair plume aye, unless turned away,
  For the tears do blind me then:
We brake no gold, a sign
  Of stronger faith to be,
But I wear his last look in my soul,
  Which said, *I love but thee !*'
     Margret, Margret.

XXIII.

IT trembled on the grass
  With a low, shadowy laughter;
And the wind did toll, as a passing soul
  Were sped by church-bell after;
And shadows, 'stead of light,
  Fell from the stars above,
In flakes of darkness on her face
  Still bright with trusting love.
     Margret, Margret.

XXIV.

' He *loved* but only thee !
  That love is transient too.

The wild hawk's bill doth dabble still
    I' the mouth that vowed thee true :
Will he open his dull eyes.
    When tears fall on his brow ?
Behold. the death-worm to his heart
    Is a nearer thing than *thou*,
           Margret, Margret.'

XXV.

Her face was on the ground—
    None saw the agony ;
But the men at sea did that night agree
    They heard a drowning cry :
And when the morning brake,
    Fast rolled the river's tide,
With the green trees waving overhead
    And a white corse laid beside.
           Margret, Margret.

XXVI.

A knight's bloodhound and he
    The funeral watch did keep ;
With a thought o' the chase he stroked its face
    As it howled to see him weep.
A fair child kissed the dead,
    But shrank before its cold.
And alone yet proudly in his hall
    Did stand a baron old.
           Margret, Margret.

XXVI.

Hang up my harp again!
  I have no voice for song.
Not song but wail, and mourners pale
  Not bards, to love belong.
  O failing human love!
    O light, by darkness known!
O false, the while thou treadest earth!
    O deaf beneath the stone!
              Margret, Margret.

ISOBEL'S CHILD.

——so find we profit,
By losing of our prayers.

SHAKESPEARE

ISOBEL'S CHILD.

I.

To rest the weary nurse has gone:
  An eight-day watch had watchëd she,
Still rocking beneath sun and moon
  The baby on her knee,
Till Isobel its mother said
'The fever waneth—wend to bed,
  For now the watch comes round to me.'

II.

Then wearily the nurse did throw
  Her pallet in the darkest place
    Of that sick room, and slept and dreamed:
For, as the gusty wind did blow
  The night-lamp's flare across her face,
    She saw or seemed to see, but dreamed,
That the poplars tall on the opposite hill,
The seven tall poplars on the hill,
Did clasp the setting sun until
His rays dropped from him, pined and still
  As blossoms in frost,
Till he waned and paled, so weirdly crossed,

To the colour of moonlight which doth pass
Over the dank ridged churchyard grass.
The poplars held the sun, and he
The eyes of the nurse that they should not see
—Not for a moment, the babe on her knee,
Though she shuddered to feel that it grew to be
Too chill, and lay too heavily.

III.

She only dreamed; for all the while
   'Twas Lady Isobel that kept
   The little baby: and it slept
Fast, warm, as if its mother's smile,
Laden with love's dewy weight,
And red as rose of Harpocrate
Dropt upon its eyelids, pressed
Lashes to cheek in a sealëd rest.

IV.

And more and more smiled Isobel
To see the baby sleep so well—
She knew not that she smiled.
Against the lattice, dull and wild
Drive the heavy droning drops,
   Drop by drop, the sound being one;
As momently time's segments fall
On the ear of God, who hears through all
   Eternity's unbroken monotone:
And more and more smiled Isobel
To see the baby sleep so well—

She knew not that she smiled.
The wind in intermission stops
  Down in the beechen forest,
    Then cries aloud
  As one at the sorest,
    Self-stung, self-driven,
And rises up to its very tops,
  Stiffening erect the branches bowed,
  Dilating with a tempest-soul
  The trees that with their dark hands break
Through their own outline, and heavy roll
  Shadows as massive as clouds in heaven
    Across the castle lake.
And more and more smiled Isobel
To see the baby sleep so well;
She knew not that she smiled;
She knew not that the storm was wild;
Through the uproar drear she could not hear
The castle clock which struck anear—
She heard the low, light breathing of her child.

          v.

O sight for wondering look!
While the external nature broke
Into such abandonment,
While the very mist, heart-rent
By the lightning, seemed to eddy
Against nature, with a din,—
A sense of silence and of steady

Natural calm appeared to come
From things without, and enter in
The human creature's room.

VI

So motionless she sate,
　The babe asleep upon her knees,
You might have dreamed their souls had gone
Away to things inanimate,
In such to live, in such to moan;
And that their bodies had ta'en back,
　In mystic change, all silences
That cross the sky in cloudy rack,
Or dwell beneath the reedy ground
In waters safe from their own sound:
Only she wore
The deepening smile I named before,
And *that* a deepening love expressed;
And who at once can love and rest?

VII.

In sooth the smile that then was keeping
Watch upon the baby sleeping,
　Floated with its tender light
Downward, from the drooping eyes,
Upward, from the lips apart,
　Over cheeks which had grown white
With an eight-day weeping:
All smiles come in such a wise

Where tears shall fall or have of old—
Like northern lights that fill the heart
Of heaven in sign of cold.

VIII.

Motionless she sate.
Her hair had fallen by its weight
On each side of her smile and lay
Very blackly on the arm
Where the baby nestled warm,
Pale as baby carved in stone
Seen by glimpses of the moon
    Up a dark cathedral aisle:
But, through the storm, no moonbeam fell
Upon the child of Isobel—
Perhaps you saw it by the ray
    Alone of her still smile.

IX.

A solemn thing it is to me
    To look upon a babe that sleeps,
    Wearing in its spirit-deeps
The undeveloped mystery
    Of our Adam's taint and woe,
Which, when they developed be,
    Will not let it slumber so;
Lying new in life beneath
The shadow of the coming death,
With that soft, low, quiet breath,

As if it felt the sun;
Knowing all things by their blooms.
Not their roots, yea, sun and sky
Only by the warmth that comes
Out of each, earth only by
    The pleasant hues that o'er it run,
And human love by drops of sweet
    White nourishment still hanging round
    The little mouth so slumber-bound:
All which broken sentiency
And conclusion incomplete,
    Will gather and unite and climb
To an immortality
    Good or evil, each sublime,
Through life and death to life again.
    O little lids, now folded fast,
    Must ye learn to drop at last
       Our large and burning tears?
O warm quick body, must thou lie,
When the time comes round to die,
    Still from all the whirl of years,
Bare of all the joy and pain?
O small frail being, wilt thou stand
At God's right hand,
Lifting up those sleeping eyes
Dilated by great destinies,
    To an endless waking? thrones and seraphim.
Through the long ranks of their solemnities,
Sunning thee with calm looks of Heaven's surprise,

But thine alone on Him?
Or else, self-willed, to tread the Godless place,
(God keep thy will!) feel thine own energies
Cold, strong, objèctless, like a dead man's clasp,
The sleepless deathless life within thee grasp,—
While myriad faces, like one changeless face,
With woe *not love's*, shall glass thee everywhere
And overcome thee with thine own despair?

x.

More soft, less solemn images
Drifted o'er the lady's heart
    Silently as snow.
She had seen eight days depart
Hour by hour, on bended knees,
    With pale-wrung hands and prayings low
And broken, through which came the sound
Of tears that fell against the ground,
Making sad stops:—'Dear Lord, dear Lord!'
She still had prayed, (the heavenly word
Broken by an earthly sigh)
—'Thou who didst not erst deny
The mother-joy to Mary mild,
Blessèd in the blessèd child
Which hearkened in meek babyhood
Her cradle-hymn, albeit used
To all that music interfused
In breasts of angels high and good!
Oh, take not, Lord, my babe away—

Oh, take not to thy songful heaven
The pretty baby thou hast given,
Or ere that I have seen him play
Around his father's knees and known
That *he* knew how my love has gone
From all the world to him.
Think, God among the cherubim,
How I shall shiver every day
In thy June sunshine, knowing where
The grave-grass keeps it from his fair
Still cheeks: and feel, at every tread,
His little body, which is dead
And hidden in thy turfy fold,
Doth make thy whole warm earth a-cold!
O God, I am so young, so young—
 I am not used to tears at nights
Instead of slumber—not to prayer
With sobbing lips and hands out-wrung!
Thou knowest all my prayings were
 'I bless thee, God, for past delights—
Thank God!' I am not used to bear
Hard thoughts of death; the earth doth cover
No face from me of friend or lover:
And must the first who teaches me
The form of shrouds and funerals, be
Mine own first-born belovèd? he
Who taught me first this mother-love?
Dear Lord who spreadest out above
Thy loving, transpiercèd hands to meet

All lifted hearts with blessing sweet,—
Pierce not my heart, my tender heart
Thou madest tender! Thou who art
So happy in thy heaven alway,
Take not mine only bliss away!'

XI.

She so had prayed: and God, who hears
Through seraph-songs the sound of tears
From that belovëd babe had ta'en
The fever and the beating pain.
And more and more smiled Isobel
To see the baby sleep so well,
    (She knew not that she smiled, I wis)
Until the pleasant gradual thought
Which near her heart the smile enwrought,
Now soft and slow, itself did seem
To float along a happy dream,
    Beyond it into speech like this.

XII.

'I prayed for thee, my little child,
    And God has heard my prayer!
And when thy babyhood is gone,
We two together undefiled
By men's repinings, will kneel down
    Upon His earth which will be fair
(Not covering thee, sweet!) to us twain,
    And give Him thankful praise.'

XIII.

Dully and wildly drives the rain:
Against the lattices drives the rain.

XIV.

'I thank Him now, that I can think
    Of those same future days,
Nor from the harmless image shrink
    Of what I there might see—
Strange babies on their mothers' knee,
Whose innocent soft faces might
From off mine eyelids strike the light,
    With looks not meant for me!'

XV.

Gustily blows the wind through the rain,
As against the lattices drives the rain.

XVI.

'But now, O baby mine, together,
We turn this hope of ours again
    To many an hour of summer weather,
When we shall sit and intertwine
    Our spirits, and instruct each other
    In the pure loves of child and mother!
Two human loves make one divine.'

XVII.

The thunder tears through the wind and the rain,
As full on the lattices drives the rain.

XVIII.

'My little child, what wilt thou choose?
  Now let me look at thee and ponder.
What gladness, from the gladnesses
  Futurity is spreading under
Thy gladsome sight?   Beneath the trees
Wilt thou lean all day, and lose
Thy spirit with the river seen
Intermittently between
  The winding beechen alleys,—
Half in labour, half repose,
  Like a shepherd keeping sheep,
  Thou, with only thoughts to keep
Which never a bound will overpass,
And which are innocent as those
  That feed among Arcadian valleys
Upon the dewy grass?

XIX.

The large white owl that with age is blind,
  That hath sate for years in the old tree hollow,
Is carried away in a gust of wind;
His wings could bear him not as fast
As he goeth now the lattice past;
  He is borne by the winds, the rains do follow,
His white wings to the blast out-flowing,
He hooteth in going,
And still, in the lightnings, coldly glitter
  His round unblinking eyes.

XX.

'Or, baby, wilt thou think it fitter
  To be eloquent and wise,
One upon whose lips the air
  Turns to solemn verities
For men to breathe anew, and win
A deeper-seated life within?
Wilt be a philosopher,
  By whose voice the earth and skies
Shall speak to the unborn?
Or a poet, broadly spreading
  The golden immortalities
Of thy soul on natures lorn
  And poor of such, them all to guard
From their decay,—beneath thy treading,
Earth's flowers recovering hues of Eden,—
And stars, drawn downward by thy looks,
To shine ascendant in thy books?'

XXI.

  The tame hawk in the castle-yard,
How it screams to the lightning, with its wet
Jagged plumes overhanging the parapet!
And at the lady's door the hound
Scratches with a crying sound.

XXII.

'But, O my babe, thy lids are laid
  Close, fast upon thy cheek,

And not a dream of power and sheen
Can make a passage up between;
Thy heart is of thy mother's made,
  Thy looks are very meek,
And it will be their chosen place
To rest on some beloved face,
  As these on thine, and let the noise
Of the whole world go on nor drown
  The tender silence of thy joys:
Or when that silence shall have grown
  Too tender for itself, the same
Yearning for sound,—to look above
And utter its one meaning, LOVE,
  That *He* may hear His name.'

XXIII.

No wind, no rain, no thunder!
The waters had trickled not slowly,
The thunder was not spent
Nor the wind near finishing;
Who would have said that the storm was
  diminishing?
No wind, no rain, no thunder!
Their noises dropped asunder
From the earth and the firmament,
From the towers and the lattices,
Abrupt and echoless
As ripe fruits on the ground unshaken wholly
    As life in death.

And sudden and solemn the silence fell,
Startling the heart of Isobel
  As the tempest could not:
Against the door went panting the breath
Of the lady's hound whose cry was still,
  And she, constrained howe'er she would not
Lifted her eyes and saw the moon
Looking out of heaven alone
  Upon the poplared hill,—
  A calm of God, made visible
  That men might bless it at their will.

XXIV.

The moonshine on the baby's face
  Falleth clear and cold;
The mother's looks have fallen back
  To the same place:
Because no moon with silver rack,
Nor broad sunrise in jasper skies
  Has power to hold
  Our loving eyes,
  Which still revert, as ever must
  Wonder and Hope, to gaze on the dust.

XXV.

The moonshine on the baby's face
  Cold and clear remaineth;
The mother's looks do shrink away,—
The mother's looks return to stay,
  As charmèd by what paineth:

Is any glamour in the case?
   Is it dream or is it sight?
Hath the change upon the wild
   Elements that signs the night,
Passed upon the child?
   It is not dream, but sight.

XXVI.

The babe has awakened from sleep
   And unto the gaze of its mother
   Bent over it, lifted another—
   Not the baby-looks that go
   Unaimingly to and fro,
But an earnest gazing deep
Such as soul gives soul at length
   When by work and wail of years
It winneth a solemn strength
   And mourneth as it wears.
A strong man could not brook
   With pulse unhurried by fears,
To meet that baby's look
   O'erglazed by manhood's tears,
The tears of a man full grown,
With a power to wring our own,
In the eyes all undefiled
Of a little three-months' child--
To see that babe-brow wrought
By the witnessing of thought
   To judgment's prodigy,

And the small soft mouth unweaned,
By mother's kiss o'erleaned,
(Putting the sound of loving
Where no sound else was moving
   Except the speechless cry)
Quickened to mind's expression,
Shaped to articulation,
Yea, uttering words, yea, naming woe,
   In tones that with it strangely went
   Because so baby-innocent,
As the child spake out to the mother, so.—

XXVII.

'O mother, mother, loose thy prayer
   Christ's name hath made it strong.
It bindeth me, it holdeth me
With its most loving cruelty,
   From floating my new soul along
   The happy heavenly air.
It bindeth me, it holdeth me
   In all this dark, upon this dull
Low earth, by only weepers trod.
It bindeth me, it holdeth me!
   Mine angel looketh sorrowful
Upon the face of God.*

XXVIII.

'Mother, mother, can I dream
   Beneath your earthly trees?

---

* For I say unto you that in Heaven their angels do always behold
the face of my Father which is in Heaven.—Matt. ch. xviii. ver. 10.

I had a vision and a gleam,
   I heard a sound more sweet than these
When rippled by the wind :
     Did you see the Dove with wings
     Bathed in golden glisterings
From a sunless light behind,
   Dropping on me from the sky,
Soft as mother's kiss, until
I seemed to leap and yet was still ?
   Saw you how His love-large eye
Looked upon me mystic calms,
    Till the power of His divine
    Vision was indrawn to mine ?

XXIX.

' Oh, the dream within the dream !
   I saw celestial places even.
Oh, the vistas of high palms
    Making finites of delight
    Through the heavenly infinite,
Lifting up their green still tops
    To the heaven of heaven !
Oh, the sweet life-tree that drops
Shade like light across the river
Glorified in its for ever
    Flowing from the Throne !
Oh, the shining holinesses
Of the thousand, thousand faces
    God-sunned by the thronèd ONE

And made intense with such a love
That though I saw them turned above,
Each loving seemed for also me!
And, oh, the Unspeakable, the HE,
The manifest in secrecies
   Yet of mine own heart partaker
With the overcoming look
Of One who hath been once forsook
   And blesseth the forsaker!
Mother, mother, let me go
Toward the Face that looketh so!
   Through the mystic wingèd Four
Whose are inward, outward eyes
Dark with light of mysteries
   And the restless evermore
'Holy, holy, holy,'—through
The sevenfold Lamps that burn in view
   Of cherubim and seraphim,—
Through the four-and-twenty crowned
Stately elders white around,
   Suffer me to go to Him!

XXX.

'Is your wisdom very wise,
   Mother, on the narrow earth,
   Very happy, very worth
That I should stay to learn?
Are these air-corrupting sighs
   Fashioned by unlearnèd breath?

Do the students' lamps that burn
   All night, illumine death?
Mother, albeit this be so,
Loose thy prayer and let me go
Where that bright chief angel stands
Apart from all his brother bands,
Too glad for smiling, having bent
In angelic wilderment
O'er the depths of God, and brought
Reeling thence one only thought
To fill his own eternity.
He the teacher is for me—
He can teach what I would know—
Mother, mother, let me go!

XXXI.

' Can your poet make an Eden
   No winter will undo,
And light a starry fire while heeding
   His hearth's is burning too?
Drown in music the earth's din,
And keep his own wild soul within
   The law of his own harmony?
Mother, albeit this be so,
Let me to my heaven go!
   A little harp me waits thereby,
A harp whose strings are golden all
And tuned to music spherical,

Hanging on the green life-tree
Where no willows ever be.
Shall I miss that harp of mine?
Mother, no!—the Eye divine
Turned upon it, makes it shine;
And when I touch it, poems sweet
Like separate souls shall fly from it,
Each to the immortal fytte.
We shall all be poets there,
Gazing on the chiefest Fair

XXXII.

' Love! earth's love! and *can* we love
Fixedly where all things move?
Can the sinning love each other?
Mother, mother,
I tremble in thy close embrace,
I feel thy tears adown my face,
    Thy prayers do keep me out of bliss
O dreary earthly love!
Loose thy prayer and let me go
    To the place which loving is
Yet not sad; and when is given
Escape to *thee* from this below,
Thou shalt behold me that I wait
For thee beside the happy Gate,
And silence shall be up in heaven
    To hear our greeting kiss.'

XXXIII.

The nurse awakes in the morning sun,
  And starts to see beside her bed
  The lady with a grandeur spread
Like pathos o'er her face, as one
God-satisfied and earth-undone;
  The babe upon her arm was dead:
And the nurse could utter forth no cry,—
She was awed by the calm in the mother's eye.

XXXIV.

' Wake, nurse!' the lady said;
  ' *We* are waking—he and I—
  I, on earth, and he, in sky:
And thou must help me to o'erlay
With garment white this little clay
  Which needs no more our lullaby.

XXXV.

' I changed the cruel prayer I made,
And bowed my meekened face, and prayed
That God would do His will; and thus
He did it, nurse! He parted us:
And His sun shows victorious
The dead calm face,—and *I* am calm,
And Heaven is hearkening a new psalm.

XXXVI.

' This earthly noise is too anear,
Too loud, and will not let me hear

The little harp.   My death will soon
Make silence.'

           And a sense of tune,
A satisfied love meanwhile
Which nothing earthly could despoil,
Sang on within her soul.

           XXXVII.

              Oh you,
Earth's tender and impassioned few,
Take courage to entrust your love
To Him so named who guards above
    Its ends and shall fulfil!
Breaking the narrow prayers that may
Befit your narrow hearts, away
    In His broad, loving will.

LONDON : PRINTED BY
SPOTTISWOODE AND CO., NEW-STREET SQUARE
AND PARLIAMENT STREET

www.ingramcontent.com/pod-product-compliance
Lightning Source LLC
Chambersburg PA
CBHW060514030726
47498CB00004B/948